Hexes and Haunts

Witch Haven Cozy Mystery - book 2

K.E. O'Connor

K.E. O'Connor Books

HEXES AND HAUNTS

Copyright © 2021 by K.E. O'Connor

ISBN: 978-1-915378-29-3

Written by: K.E. O'Connor

Preface

The Witch Haven series has been created so you spend time with four amazing witches:

Books 1-3 tell Indigo's story: Spells and Spooks, Hexes and Haunts, Curses and Corpses

Books 4-6 tell Luna's story: Muffins and Moonlight, Cupcakes and Cauldrons, Pancakes and Potions

Book 7-9 tell Odessa's story: Hauntings and High Jinx, Hauntings and Havoc, Hauntings and Hoaxes

Book 10-12 tell Storm's story: The Case of the Screaming Skull, The Case of the Poisoned Pumpkin, The Case of the Cursed Candy

And there are two bonus origin stories to enjoy: **Fire Fang** and **Silvaria**

Chapter 1

Is it possible to kill someone with a cupcake? As I eyed the desserts in front of me with suspicion, I figured it most definitely was.

"Those are the worst cakes I've ever seen. It looks like you've squashed a gnome and covered it in ghost goo." Nugget, my cat familiar, was perched on top of a kitchen cabinet, looking down at me with disdain on his furry face.

I frowned at the misshapen, sunken cupcakes covered in gray icing. "How did I get a simple baking spell so wrong? I can't give these to Albert to sell in the bakery. His customers will think he's trying to poison them."

My spider familiar, Hilda, ran up my leg and tapped the back of my hand with one hairy limb. "It's the effort that counts. He'll appreciate them."

"That's not true in this case," Nugget said. "You can't take those things to the bakery. You'll give Albert a heart attack, and he's stressed out enough as it is."

"I'm trying to be helpful. I don't know why I bothered." I picked up the tray of a dozen ugly cupcakes and walked to the trash.

Russell, my other familiar, soared over my head, flapping his wings and cawing unhappily.

"You can't want to eat these," I said to him.

He settled on the countertop and bobbed his head.

I set down the cupcakes. They definitely weren't something anyone in their right mind would buy, but they probably tasted okay. And I didn't mind gray icing, so long as I closed my eyes and didn't think of ghost slime.

I glanced at the cauldron bubbling on the stove. It would be ten more minutes before the location spell was at full strength. That gave me enough time to have a quick cup of coffee and try my baking.

I switched on the kettle and pulled out a mug and a tub of instant coffee.

"You're really going to eat one of those monstrosities?" Nugget said.

"We all are. After all, you're my familiars. It's your job to protect me from anything potentially deadly."

"I'm not protecting you from your own terrible baking," Nugget said.

Russell bobbed nearer to the cakes, an eager look in his beady black eyes.

"Russell loves my baking, don't you?" I stroked his silky black wings.

"He's only interested in them because he thinks they look like giant toads," Nugget said.

"My cakes don't look like..." When I squinted my eyes, they did sort of look like misshapen amphibians. "Okay, so baking spells aren't my forte. I'm still getting the hang of all this extra power."

I lifted my hands and admired the sparkle shifting across the surface of my palms.

It had only been a few days since I'd reacquired my full witch powers, and a little extra boost, and I was adjusting. And as the cakes demonstrated, my adjustment wasn't going so well.

I pulled out a plate and set a cupcake on it.

We all looked at it. No one made the first move to take a bite.

I grabbed a knife and cut it into four pieces. "Let's do this together."

"Count me out," Nugget said. "I don't want to get sick."

"I'll try some," Hilda said, from her favorite position on my shoulder.

"My cakes can't be any worse than eating all those flies you love so much," I said.

"Flies are delicious," Hilda said. "You can't beat them. But I'll try a bit of cake now and again. How about you, Russell?"

Russell hopped from foot to foot.

I lifted a piece of cupcake up to Nugget, but he wrinkled his nose and hissed at me.

"You need to work on your familiar skills," I said to him. "Hilda and Russell have gotten into the swing of it."

He stood, turned in a circle and settled back down so he was looking at the wall.

I grinned, despite his crabby behavior. I still felt lucky Nugget, Hilda, and Russell had accepted me as their witch. After abandoning them for more than a decade, they had every right to turn their beaks and noses up at me and find someone else to support in her witching duties. But they'd stuck by my side and helped me in times of trouble. I'd be eternally grateful to them. Although I wouldn't be baking them any thank you cakes anytime soon.

I made my coffee, took a few sips, then lifted a piece of cupcake. I took a bite. It tasted of... nothing. It didn't taste sweet or sour. It was just bland. I swallowed the cake.

Everyone was looking at me as if they expected me to keel over and foam at the mouth.

"It wasn't that bad," I said. "Go on, you two, you haven't tried your pieces yet."

Russell grabbed his cake and swallowed it in one go.

Hilda scuttled onto the counter and took a tiny bite of cupcake.

A few seconds later, Russell heaved up a soggy lump of cake. He shook out his wings and backed away.

"Oh dear! Was it really that terrible?" I said.

He cawed mournfully, before flapping up to his perch in the corner of the kitchen.

Hilda backed away from the rest of the cake. "Hmmm, the trash is the best place for them. Let's forget about the baking. We can help Albert much more by finding Luna."

I pointed at the cauldron. "That's what the spell is for. I needed a distraction whilst it was maturing, otherwise I'd have kept tinkering."

My best friend, Luna Brimstone, had been taken from her hospital bed while recovering from an attack by a malevolent ghost. I'd promised her Uncle Albert that I'd get her back, especially since

I'd aggravated the ghost who most likely took her. But so far, I'd had no luck. This location spell was my latest attempt at finding out where Luna was.

With a sigh of regret, I tossed the cakes into the trash, then headed to the large oak kitchen table where I'd laid out a huge map of the local area.

The village of Witch Haven was small, home to six hundred and sixty-six magic users. That number always stayed the same. Although it had temporarily changed when I was seventeen and was seduced by dark magic, alongside my wonderful stepmom, Magda. We'd wiped out ten percent of the population in a single day.

I tried not to dwell on that too much. It wasn't my finest hour.

I studied the map of the village. The house I lived in was set along a quiet dirt track, close to the forest. It was a perfect, secluded location for a witch in hiding. And that was definitely my tag. Although I was working on changing that.

And one step to doing so, was to find my missing best friend and prove to the Magic Council I was no longer a black magic using witch, and had a positive reason for being in the village.

"Check to see if the spell is ready." Hilda was perched on my shoulder again.

I walked over and gave the liquid a stir. It shimmered from orange to green. That was a sign the ingredients had mixed and the locator spell was active.

I used a small ladle to decant the spell and headed back to the map.

Russell hopped onto the table from his perch and stood to one side of the map. Nugget shuffled around to watch, then yawned and closed his eyes. I knew he was interested in what was going on, he just pretended not to care.

I used a pipette to extract some of the spell and held it over the map. I took a deep breath and attempted to channel my power. The troubling factor in this spell casting game of chance was that it wasn't entirely my own power I was using, so the channeling wasn't always spot on.

Before my stepmom had died, she'd left behind a number of magically charged items in this house. I was wearing her amethyst necklace, which supercharged my own ability to such an extent that I often sparked magic without even realizing what I was doing.

I raised one hand, closed my eyes, and centered myself. I imagined Luna, her warm, mischievous smile and the way she always greeted me with a bone crunching hug.

I was blessed to still have her as my best friend. Even after everything that had gone down, she was steadfast and loyal. And she was the first to come find me when I returned to Witch Haven under a cloud of darkness.

Now it was my turn to help her.

I dispensed three drops of the spell onto the map. I opened my eyes and watched as they rolled onto the paper like tiny pearls. Rather than sinking into the map, they shifted around, seeking out my missing friend.

When the spell worked, the three drops would merge on the spot where Luna could be found.

After ten minutes of waiting and watching, the drops of liquid stopped in opposite corners of the map.

"Are you sure you mixed the ingredients right?" Nugget said.

"Positive. You all watched me do it," I said.

"This is a good sign," Hilda said. "If Luna was dead, the liquid wouldn't have moved at all."

"Or it would have sunk into the graveyard," Nugget said.

The liquid hovered, as if it was about to move, but was uncertain where to go.

"It's showing you Luna's not anywhere," Hilda said.

"That can't be right. She must be somewhere. A witch doesn't just vanish without a trace."

We were all quiet as we continued to stare at the map.

"She could have been taken into a limbo-like place," Hilda said. "The place ghosts lurk when they have nothing better to do."

"I get stuck there each time I die," Nugget said. "It's not that much fun."

I grimaced. He was still reminding me of the time I'd accidentally buried him when I thought he'd died. Nugget was magically charged, so could regenerate if ever something fatal happened to him. He was a cat with not just nine lives, but potentially an infinite number of lives, thanks to Magda's magic that kept him alive.

"You can't take a living person into limbo," I said.

"Luna could be unconscious," Hilda said. "That would give her a foot between two worlds. The ghost who has her—"

"If it's even that mean ghost from her apartment," I said. "We still haven't figured out who took her for certain."

"Yes, but if it is that ghost, he's powerful. We barely survived when we went up against him. He could be holding her there. And it seems logical it would be him. Who else would want to harm Luna? She's a sweetie."

I threw my hands up in frustration. A blast of magic shot out of one palm and smashed a hole straight through the ceiling. I ducked as plaster rained down on me.

I lowered my hands and stared at them. "Sorry, house. I still don't know my own strength."

The kitchen door slammed in response. It wasn't only the residents of Witch Haven who had magic. This amazing house was a little special, too. And it didn't like it when I blasted a hole through important things like ceilings.

I hurried out of the kitchen and dashed upstairs to assess the damage. The magic had not only blasted through the floor, it had also gone through the roof. I could see daylight through the not insignificant hole.

I stopped by the window and looked outside. My eyes widened, and I grabbed the window ledge. Olympus Duke, Head of the Magic Council, stood by the pile of rubble next to my house.

Nugget hopped onto the window ledge and growled. "He's still not leaving us alone. He's been back every day since you escaped."

"He can't know this house is still here," I whispered. "The magic wards are keeping it concealed."

"Olympus is a strong magic user." Hilda ran up my leg. "Maybe he can sense the wards, but can't figure out where the magic is coming from."

"Or he can sense you," Nugget said. "Especially if you keep smashing magic through the roof of a hidden house. We won't stay hidden for long if you keep misfiring your spells."

I wrinkled my nose. The Magic Council wanted me for lots of reasons. I owed them money, and I'd escaped their custody after being arrested for the illegal use of magic. Plus, I was hiding in a house they thought they'd destroyed. They had plans to turn me into a shadow and remove my magic. But there was no way I was letting that happen. My life was getting back on track, and I wasn't having it torn away because the Magic Council couldn't see sense. Witches could change. I was living proof.

And if that wasn't enough of a problem, I had to get Luna back. I owed it to her. And I owed it to her uncle. If the Magic Council got in my way, things would turn nasty. But my friend's safety meant the world to me. If getting her back put the Magic Council's pompous noses out of joint, then so be it. I'd deal with the consequences when they finally caught up with me.

"We need to give the Magic Council something else to worry about," I said. "Surely, I can't be the only witch they're interested in. There must be some other badly behaving magic user out there they can target."

"I've got a plan to deal with Olympus and his minions." Nugget hopped off the window ledge.

"What are you going to do?" I asked.

"I've been meaning to try out some diversion magic. There are a few spells I've been studying in Magda's books. They could be fun to use on Olympus."

"What kind of diversions are we talking about?" I said. "You don't want the Magic Council chasing you, too."

"If they do, I can escape them. I'm fast on my furry paws. A few spells cast around the village will keep them busy, and they'll forget all about you." Nugget bounded down the stairs before I had a chance to stop him and learn more.

I looked at Hilda. "Why's he suddenly being so helpful?"

"Because even though he doesn't like to tell you, he's happy you're back and have decided to stay. He was miserable with no witch to claim as his own."

I smiled to myself. I could get used to this life. I'd only been back in Witch Haven a short time, but it already felt like home again, and I was planning on staying put. So long as I could prevent the Magic Council from stripping me of my witch abilities. Oh yes, and get rid of my debts, figure out a way to keep this house, and locate my missing best friend.

I spotted Nugget out the window, scurrying away in the opposite direction to Olympus.

Olympus didn't see him. Instead, he knelt and placed something on the ground before leaving.

"What's he up to?" I muttered. Anything the Magic Council left for me to find was never going to be good. The last time he visited, he'd brought a list of debts I needed to repay.

"Send Russell out to get it," Hilda said. "He's fast on the wing. If anyone is watching, they'll just see a black blur zoom past."

I headed back down the stairs with her and directed Russell out the front door to grab whatever Olympus had left behind.

He sped back a moment later with a piece of rolled paper gripped between his talons.

I extracted it and unrolled it. It had a single sentence on it. *We need to talk.*

My gut clenched, and I shook my head. How did he know I was here? Everyone believed the house was gone, so why was he coming back and leaving messages for me to find?

"This could be a positive thing," Hilda said. "Olympus is softening toward you. And we need him as an ally."

"Olympus Duke won't ever be my ally. He was the one who arrested me and locked me away almost as soon as I returned to Witch Haven."

"Maybe Albert has put in a good word for you," Hilda said. "He must have told Olympus you've been helping to find Luna. And you did banish those ghosts from her apartment."

"I banished one." I gestured at the ghost jar containing the trapped ghost that sat on Magda's magic cabinet. "But I let the other go. No, I can't trust Olympus. We don't need him involved with this. He'll only interfere. And there's no way the Head of the Magic Council will bend the rules, and that's what we need to do to get Luna back."

I headed back into the kitchen, finished my coffee, and then tried the location spell three more times. I got exactly the same results. The liquid zoomed around the map for several minutes, before the three separate drops hovered in the corners.

I dispersed the spell and rolled up the map. "We need to try something else. There must be a spell to show me where Luna is."

A loud thudding on the front door had me jumping.

Russell squawked and flew out of the kitchen.

Hilda clung to my shoulder. "That sounds like someone is in a bad mood. If they keep thumping so hard, they'll knock down the door," she whispered.

"It doesn't sound friendly. But how has that someone found the front door to bang on in the first place?" I crept toward the door and peered cautiously through a window beside it.

Ursa Wyrm stood outside, her lips pressed together as she clasped a squirming Nugget to her chest.

Chapter 2

I ducked back from the window, but was a second too late as Ursa turned and saw me.

She thumped on the door again. "Don't hide from me, Indigo Ash. I know this mangy cat belongs to you."

"How is she seeing the house?" I whispered to Hilda.

"I don't know, but you need to let her in, or she'll keep thumping on the door and give the game away. If Olympus was around when she arrived, he'd have followed her right here."

I stared at my hands. Was my magic failing me again? I'd only just got it back, and it was already malfunctioning. I shook my head. There must be some other reason Ursa could see the house when no one else could.

"Open up this instant, or I'm taking this cat and having him stuffed for my mantelpiece," Ursa said in a high-pitched nasal voice.

"You'd better open the door," Hilda said. "I hate the thought of Nugget being stuffed. Although at least it would stop his complaining."

"It probably wouldn't. He'd still find a way to let us know he was grumpy about something." I grabbed the handle, unlocked it, and pulled open the door.

Ursa was a tall woman, standing at well over six-feet tall. She had her hair scraped back in a tight bun set at the base of her neck and wore an unflattering calf-length flower print dress.

Before she had a chance to say a word, I grabbed her arm, yanked her into the hallway, and slammed the door shut. "How did you get through my magic?"

Ursa arched a thin gray eyebrow. "You're not the only one with power around here. I believe this thing is yours." She held out Nugget.

I grabbed him from her. "He is. Why do you have him?"

"Ursa's creepy old house was my diversion plan." Nugget squirmed out of my grip and landed elegantly on the floor.

"My beautiful house isn't creepy," Ursa said. "How dare you."

I remembered Ursa's house. Imagine the scariest movie style house you've ever seen. Times that by ten. Then add creepy corner turrets, narrow windows that were lead-lined and smoky so you couldn't see in, curtains that twitched on their own, and strange smells drifting from a garden that stank of the dead. That was Ursa's house. It was called Gravesend Manor.

"What were you doing creeping about in Ursa's house?" I said to Nugget.

"I wasn't in the house, just the garden. She has those nasty gnomes dotted about. I was planning to bring them to life and set them to work on the village. They'd be the perfect distraction for the Magic Council."

"Don't you put one paw on my gnomes. They're precious to me," Ursa said. "And why would you want to bring them alive any more than they already are?"

"Your garden gnomes are alive?" I said.

"Of course they are. But that's beside the point." Her stony stare fixed on to Nugget. "What are you going to do about your misbehaving cat? I can't allow him in my garden. I expect he does his business in there as well as trying to interfere with my gnomes. Cats have no ideas about boundaries. No pooping on my flowers."

"All your flowers are already dead," Nugget said. "Some of my fertilizer would revive them."

I held up a hand to stop the bickering from going any further. "You still haven't told me how you got through my magic wards. How were you able to see this house?"

Ursa narrowed her eyes at me. "I knew Magda well."

"Which doesn't answer my question. No one should be able to see this place."

"Perhaps not. But I'm powerful." She sniffed and lifted her chin. "I take it you're hiding from someone."

"Yes! From everyone."

Ursa looked around the hallway. "This place hasn't changed much since the last time I was here. It was only a few weeks before Magda went dark."

"I haven't gotten around to updating yet," I said. "I've been busy."

"Yes, the entire village has been talking about your unwelcome return." Ursa marched past me and entered the living room.

"Make yourself at home, why don't you." It looked like she wasn't leaving anytime soon. I followed Ursa, along with Nugget and Hilda.

Russell was perched in the corner of the living room. He squawked when he saw Ursa and disappeared into the kitchen.

She turned to face me. "I knew Magda and I know this house. I also recognized Nugget when he turned up in my garden, and I figured something was wrong. I heard what the Magic Council did to the house, so decided to take a look. It didn't take me long to discover the magic wards, but then I often combined magic with Magda when we worked a big job together, so her magic felt familiar."

"I didn't know you worked together." I gestured to a chair, eager to hear more about Magda before she turned dark. That was all people were interested in talking about, and there was so much more to her than that.

Ursa perched on the seat. "We did. I liked her. And even when she went rogue, I fought her corner for a while, but the evidence was insurmountable. She let dark magic take over, and you followed in her footsteps. This village will never forget what you did."

I settled in the seat opposite her. "That's why I'm still here. Well, it's one of the reasons I'm staying in Witch Haven. Magda was innocent. So am I. And I'm going to prove that."

"I expect all criminals say that."

"Maybe so, but I have evidence."

Ursa tilted her head. "Even though I didn't lose anyone the day you two attacked, I remember it well. You were blasting out that toxic magic like glitter from a unicorn's backside. It's amazing more people weren't killed."

"We didn't do that willingly." I clasped my hands together, my magic tickling my skin. "And I'm going to clear Magda's name. I'll show she wasn't responsible for her actions that day."

"Tell me how you expect to do that, when everyone saw what happened to her?" Ursa settled back in her seat.

"Um, I don't have the time right now. Perhaps we could arrange—"

"I'm not leaving until I know why you're here and what your plans are. If I get a hint you're plotting more trouble, I'll take you down myself." She folded her arms across her narrow chest. "And you can make me a herbal tea. Call it payment for bringing that mangy furball back to you alive."

Nugget must have slipped out of the room, because he was nowhere to be seen to defend himself. I bet he was listening in, and would be furious at being called mangy. He spent hours grooming his fur until it shone.

"We can do tea another time. I really have to—"

"You really have to convince me you're not here to cause trouble. Or I'll go straight to the Magic Council. I'm sure you're aware they're looking for you."

"No! Don't do that. I'm here for genuine reasons. If you really were Magda's friend, you wouldn't turn me in."

"And I won't, so long as you explain yourself." She studied me as she peered down her long nose. "How about this? You answer my questions, and I'll answer yours. And if I'm satisfied with your responses, I'll even show you how to secure the magic wards around the house so no one will ever find this place."

"You're on." That was an offer I couldn't refuse. I swiftly made two mugs of peppermint tea, grabbed cookies from a packet, and returned to the living room.

Ursa stood by Magda's magic cabinet, one hand resting on it.

I set down the tray with the drinks and cookies on and walked over to her.

"We cast blindingly impressive spells thanks to the contents of this cabinet." She patted the cabinet like it was her favorite gnome. "Tell me why you think Magda is innocent?"

We returned to our seats, and I took a sip of my herbal tea. I wasn't a hundred percent sure about sharing everything with Ursa, but she could be useful to me, and I needed to keep her on side.

"Magda kept journals when she was alive. They contained everything from spells she was trying through to her thoughts about what happened on a particular day. She kept them in that cabinet. I pulled one out and discovered she'd left me a message inside it. It told me a rival witch coven wanted to take over Witch Haven. They used

Magda to do that and threatened my life. They forced her to act the way she did. She tried to keep her grip on the magic they gave her, but it got out of control. It infected me, too."

Ursa lifted her mug and took a sip. "I've always wondered about that day. It was so out of character for Magda. Although a few weeks before it happened, she became withdrawn. She turned down several invitations to try a new spell I'd been working on. It was unlike her. She was always on the cutting edge of magic because of you."

"Me? What did I have to do with her testing spells?"

"Magda wanted to stay a step ahead of you, so she could help you if you ever needed it." Ursa shook her head. "She was so fond of you."

My throat tightened. "Magda was much more powerful than me."

"Because you hadn't come into your full power. The day you turned eighteen, that would have changed. Of course, you got yourself arrested by the Magic Council, so your true potential was hampered. But Magda wanted to ensure she could provide you with a proper mentorship."

I blinked away tears as happy memories of Magda threatened to overwhelm me. "She was always great to me. And now I have her journals. They've opened my eyes to the possibility someone else was behind what happened all those years ago. That's my first step to clearing her name and mine. But I'm not only here for that."

Ursa tilted her head like a curious owl. "Indeed. What else keeps you here? The Magic Council want your hide. I think they've questioned just about everyone to discover your whereabouts. You've caused a stir since you returned."

"And I know it. But I'm not leaving until Luna has been found. She's my best friend. I need to make sure she's safe."

The stern expression on Ursa's face softened a fraction. "I heard about that. Is it true she wasn't well and walked out of the hospital? Some people are saying she ran away."

"She wasn't well, but she didn't run off anywhere."

"So what happened to her?"

"Luna was having trouble with a ghost. I tried to get rid of it, but only made things worse. And I've got no proof yet, but I'm certain this ghost is behind her disappearance."

Ursa's eyes narrowed. "Are you telling the truth?"

"Of course. Why would I lie about my best friend going missing?"

"Because you have a terrible reputation around here. Is it a coincidence that you show up and Luna disappears? What's to say you didn't make her vanish? Could you be the same dark witch who's trying to fool everyone again?" Ursa stiffened in her seat, and the floor beneath my feet trembled as her magic drifted around her.

"No! I've changed. Something much darker than me is troubling Witch Haven."

"I doubt that's possible. Or have you forgotten how many people died at your hand?"

I lowered my gaze. "I remember each one of them every day. But I'm not the one spreading darkness through Witch Haven."

"There's no darkness in Witch Haven. Not since you and Magda were taken away." Ursa sniffed. "I was wrong to come here. I should have gone to the Magic Council the second I discovered this place was still standing. You're the cause of our problems."

Panic welled up inside me. My fingers twitched, and I had to repress the urge to use my magic to silence Ursa. "I'm not. And don't go to the Magic Council. If you do, I'll have no chance to clear Magda's name, and no way to help Luna. I don't care what happens to me after I've fixed those problems, but I need to be free to investigate. You can report me to the Magic Council after I've made things right."

Ursa's fierce gaze remained fixed on me as she continued to drink her tea. She lowered her mug. "I have an ability few people know about. I can drain the power from a spell. Not all spells, but many of them. That's how I saw through your wards. I recognized the magic signature as that of an Ash witch. I felt around for a while and decided to see what would happen if I absorbed the spell's energy."

"That was risky. You could have been absorbing anything."

"It's not such a risk for me."

I nodded. That meant Ursa was powerful. I needed to tread carefully around this sharp-faced witch, or I'd be on the receiving end of that magic.

"I don't use it often. It's a tiring business, holding another witch's power, and my ability would be in high demand if others knew what I could do. Magda knew about it."

I kept quiet, uncertain why Ursa was telling me this.

She continued. "I keep the power of the spell temporarily. I will use that to strengthen your wards, along with a few other spells I've channeled over the last few days. No one will find you with the assistance of my magic."

"Well... thanks. I'd appreciate that." I clenched my hands around my mug. "Why help me, though? You don't trust me. You think I'm trouble."

Ursa pursed her lips. "I don't trust you completely, but I won't say anything about you being here for now. It seems you have a purpose for staying in Witch Haven. I respect that."

"Thank you. Hopefully, I'll be able to find Luna quickly. Then I can concentrate on clearing Magda's name."

"Wait, you haven't heard me out. You don't get my power for free. I believe you've always had a way with ghosts, haven't you?"

"That's right. I mean, I can see them and interact with most of them." Where was she going with this?

"I remember you as a child spending hours wandering around the graves talking to the dead. I always thought you were an odd little thing."

"It's always come naturally to me," I said. "Although I'm out of practice, I still see them as easily as I see you."

"Excellent. That's what I thought. So, here's the deal. I'll keep quiet about your hidden house and strengthen your wards, if you help me with a little problem."

"What's the problem?"

"Since you're so into ghosts, let's see what you can do about mine."

Chapter 3

I stared at Ursa. "You have a ghost problem?"

"I do. At least, I have an unwelcome presence in my home causing me trouble. It's most likely a restless spirit." She stood and headed to the front door. "Hurry up! What are you waiting for?"

I remained in my seat. "Maybe you missed the part when we talked about me being wanted by the Magic Council? I can't go wandering about with you. Olympus Duke has already been around here looking for me." Besides, I had enough going on. I couldn't add another problem to my list.

"It's already getting late, and the Magic Council don't enjoy paying overtime. Olympus is probably tucked up in his rooms already, sipping whiskey and plotting your downfall."

I shook my head. "I can look into your ghost problem another time. I must focus on finding Luna."

Ursa put her hand on the doorknob. "I understand. If you're not interested in helping, then I have no reason to keep your house a secret. Perhaps the next time Olympus asks me where you are, I'll lead him here. In fact, that's an excellent idea. It'll be good to have something over the Magic Council. They'll owe me a favor if I tell them where you've been hiding."

"No! Don't tell them I'm here." Despite everything I'd just told her, Ursa was mean enough to turn me over to them. "I'll come with you."

"I knew you'd see sense. And as a special favor, I'll go out first and ensure none of those officious Magic Council members are lurking in the bushes. And I'll see to those wards while I'm about it." She chuckled to herself as she headed out the door.

Nugget reappeared, thrashing his tail from side to side. "We're not helping that harridan. She squeezed me so tightly, I almost passed out. She's mean. And she smells of mothballs and death."

"Ursa has us backed into a corner. If we don't help her, we're in trouble. And you took a risk by lurking in her garden and messing with her gnomes. You know what she's like."

"So this is all my fault?"

I glanced at Hilda, who shook her whole body at me. "Well, you did stir her up by prodding her gnomes."

"I was helping! I thought the gnomes would be a fun idea," Nugget said. "Ursa must have an alarm set up in her garden. The second I touched one, there she was, looming over me."

"And now she's found us," I said. "And I guarantee that if we don't play her ghost game, then we're history. She'll go straight to the Magic Council and tell them everything she knows."

Hilda scuttled onto my shoulder. "What are we going to do?"

"I can't fail Luna. And I have to stay free from the Magic Councils clutches."

Nugget groaned. "We're going to Ursa's creepy house, aren't we?"

"Yes, all of us. Maybe her ghost problem will be an easy fix. We can deal with it and guarantee her silence." I held my arm out for Russell to land on, then we headed out the door.

I spotted Ursa by the gate. She turned and gave me a thumbs up. "It's all clear. It's unlikely you'll get arrested tonight. This way."

"Could she had said that any louder? I don't think the poltergeist in the last cottage on the left before you leave the village heard her," Nugget said.

"I'm sure she could. But let's not wait around to test that theory." I had to jog to catch up with Ursa as she strode along in her practical black shoes. "How long have you had this ghost problem?"

"Two days. I woke in the middle of the night and discovered my bedroom was cold. I knew it wasn't a problem with the heating. I tried the light, but it wouldn't switch on. Then a pair of glowing red eyes appeared over the end of my bed."

"This has never happened before?"

She waved a hand in the air. "There are always interesting things going on in the house. It's almost six-hundred years old, so it's bound to pick up a few misbehaving spirits from time to time. But nothing like this. And the house was built on an old burial site, which stimulates the spirits during particular phases of the moon."

Nugget shuddered. "This is going to be a nightmare. I can sense it."

Ursa glared at him.

I hurried on, sensing these two would never get along. "The place has been haunted for as long as you've lived there?"

"It has. The family records show ghosts make a regular appearance. But we know not to be afraid of such things."

"So why does this new arrival bother you?"

"This entity is different. It feels evil. Every time I sense his presence, I get cold and feel unwell. I weaken and get the shivers."

"That's because you're living in a draughty house," Nugget muttered.

"I could do with a few more draft excluders tucked at the base of my doors. If you're a willing volunteer, I'll turn you into a new furry draft excluder." Ursa reached for Nugget, her eyes glinting with malice.

He dodged out of her reach and hissed a warning.

"Hey! No threatening my familiars, or we won't help you," I said.

Nugget flicked his tail, his fur fluffed out and his gaze fixed on Ursa.

She smirked as her gaze traveled from Nugget, to Hilda, and finally to Russell. "You have three familiars. How did that come about?"

"I inherited them from Magda. They came with the house, and I now own it, so we adopted each other."

"It's most unusual for a witch to have so many familiars. It suggests you have great power. I'm not so sure myself." Ursa leaned closer and sniffed me.

"There's something unpleasant exuding from you. It's possibly a whiff of the darkness you let in."

I resisted the urge to sniff test my armpits. I knew how twisted my past was, but I didn't think it made me stink.

We walked along in silence for a few minutes. Was it a coincidence Ursa's troubles started only two days ago? That was when I'd chased the ghost out of Luna's apartment. I'd hoped I'd banished it, but perhaps all I'd done was enrage it. Maybe it was now setting its sights on other villagers.

I glanced at Ursa. It must be one heck of a powerful ghost to think it could go up against her and win.

"Follow me along the garden path. And don't annoy the gnomes. They hate strangers." Ursa pushed open a creaking set of black gates and marched in ahead of us.

Hilda clung tightly to my left shoulder, while Russell rested on the other one. Nugget stayed close to my ankles as we hurried along a path which was overgrown with looming oak trees.

"There's something watching us," Hilda whispered. "Over to the left."

"It's probably just a gnome," I said.

"Its eyes are glowing," Hilda said.

Russell squawked and flapped his wings.

"Calm down, everyone. So long as we stay close to Ursa, we'll be fine. She'll keep her killer gnomes away from us." At least, I hoped she would.

We emerged from the trees to find ourselves outside Gravesend Manor. There were no lights on in the house, despite it being late, and the front door squeaked open and closed on hinges that sounded like they needed a good oiling.

"Do you always leave your front door unlocked?" I said.

"Of course. Apart from your cat, who'd be foolish enough to try to break in and take anything from me?"

Something hard whacked me on the calf, and I yelped. I turned around to find a small stone axe by my foot. I picked it up and examined it.

"Give that to me," Ursa said. "It's just my garden guardians making sure you're not here to cause trouble."

"You mean the killer gnomes," Nugget said.

"They only kill when they're provoked or threatened, or it's a full moon." Ursa hunted in the bushes for a moment, before leaning in and pulling something out. She held up a small grubby stone gnome with a chipped red conical hat. His expression was contorted into one of rage, and one fist was curled and pointed in my direction.

"Thank you for your service, Digger. Indigo and her familiars are my guests. They're here to deal with the ghost problem. No attacking them until I give the word."

"Which you won't be giving, I hope," I said.

Ursa gave the gnome his stone axe, before setting him back on the ground. "Providing you get rid of this ghost, then we'll have no problems."

That was hardly reassuring. "I make no guarantees. I have no idea what we're dealing with."

There was a rumble of thunder overhead.

"It's not supposed to storm tonight, is it?" Nugget said.

"I'm just displeased with you," Ursa said. "Come inside before you get struck by lightning."

"Ursa caused that thunder?" Hilda whispered.

"It seems I'm not the only witch around here who knows how to manipulate the elements," I muttered. "We need to keep on Ursa's good side."

"No, what we need to do is make a run for it while we can," Nugget said. "What's to say she's not going to get us inside that creepy house and then bury us in the basement? Or give us to the gnomes at the next full moon?"

"If she buries us in the basement, you'd dig yourself out and get revenge for us all, like a good familiar should," I said.

"It depends what mood I'm in when I resurrect. I might leave you all there to rot and claim Magda's house as my own."

I wouldn't put it past Nugget to do just that, especially since I'd been feeding him value store cat food recently, which he hated.

"Come along. No dawdling." Ursa pushed open the front door and headed into a wide, dark wood paneled hallway.

I took a deep breath and stepped over the threshold. It was cold inside the house. Colder than outside. My breath fogged as I breathed out.

"Is it usually this chilly in here?"

"I like to keep things cool. It helps me have a clear head. But since the ghost arrived, things have become a little too cold for my liking," Ursa said.

I hurried past numerous large oil paintings of stern-faced family members and followed Ursa up the creaking wooden staircase to the second floor.

"The eyes on that painting just moved," Nugget said. "It's watching us."

I glanced at the painting of a bald man wearing a velvet suit and a red silk cravat. "It's probably just an artist's trick." I jumped as the eyes darted to me. "Or maybe not. Let's not hang around to find out if this painting is possessed."

"This whole house feels like it needs cleansing," Hilda said. "That could be the problem. There are too many negative energies in here and it's built up, and manifested into something cold and ill-spirited."

"An exorcism, a deep clean, and some modern furniture. That would fix the problems in this cob-webbed filled nightmare," Nugget said.

"Where do you feel the ghost energy the strongest?" I said to Ursa.

"It's been appearing in my bedroom, but I've had experiences in several other rooms. Most recently, in my collection room. That's where it lingers the most. I've had several unpleasant experiences in that space."

"What do you collect?" I said.

"Porcelain dolls."

I grimaced and shuddered. Of course, Ursa had to have a room full of dolls skulking about in the shadows and waiting for a chance to creep up on me.

"You'd better show me that room. We'll start there and see how we get on."

Something black darted out of the shadows in front of me and launched itself into the room to my right.

I stumbled back as a whiff of decay filled my nose. "Have you got a cat?"

"No. There are no cats living here."

"I just saw something run past. It looked a lot like a cat."

"Oh, it could be one of the ghost cats. Once they move in here, they never want to leave, even when they're dead. Follow me. My collection room is up ahead, on the right."

I dashed after Ursa and waited as she pulled a small key out of her pocket and unlocked the collection room door.

She turned to me. "You must be careful in this room. I've grown this collection over decades, and some of the dolls have been handed down from family members. They hold great sentimental value and are also worth a lot of money. Only touch one if you absolutely have to. And ask permission before moving anything. There are cotton gloves inside you must wear if you handle the dolls. I don't want you to leave your skin grease on my angels."

"Understood. Don't touch the creepy dolls."

Ursa's top lip curled. "And show some respect. This collection is one-of-a-kind." She pushed open the door.

I stepped inside, and my jaw dropped. Multiple rows of shelving covered the walls, and every space was crammed full with dolls. "There must be at least five hundred dolls in here."

"Six hundred and two," Ursa said proudly.

"And they're all staring at us," Hilda whispered. "We could still make a run for it."

Nugget strutted into the room. "I'm not afraid of these ugly, haunted dolls. What's the worst they can do to me?"

"Capture you, strap a saddle on your back, and ride you around until you collapse with exhaustion?" I said. "Skin you, eat you, and then stuff what's left of you and use it as a toy. Or—"

Ursa tutted. "My dolls don't misbehave. Or they didn't until two days ago."

"They're only dolls," Nugget said. "Look at the size of you compared to them. What does it matter if they misbehave?"

"They may be small, but they're mighty in number," Ursa said. "Never underestimate my marvelous dolls." She stroked the hair of a redhead porcelain doll, whose expression suggested she wanted to commit evil at the earliest opportunity.

I studied the mass of angry, bitter faces and took a step back. "You need to get someone else to look at this. I'm not all that into dolls. And if one of them is possessed, it could be too much for me to handle. I've never dealt with a possessed toy before."

"These aren't toys. These are treasures," Ursa said.

"Even so, someone who doesn't get the chills just looking at them would be better equipped to help you. Who else have you spoken to about your doll issue?"

"Given your dark leanings, you were the first person I thought of. And as an Ash witch, this should be a simple task." Ursa pressed her lips together. "Unless, of course, you have no interest in keeping your whereabouts hidden from the Magic Council."

So, I had two lousy options in front of me. Get blackmailed by Ursa and face off with the evil dolls, or risk getting arrested by the Magic Council. Neither choice was great.

"You've got this." Nugget nudged me with his head. "They're just dumb dolls."

Russell squawked his agreement, but had yet to leave my shoulder, suggesting he didn't think much of the dolls either.

"If you don't think you're witch enough for this job, I'll simply get in touch with the Magic Council and be done with you," Ursa said. "No one wants a useless witch to remain in the village. Especially not one with such a bad reputation. But if you help me, it could be looked on favorably. And I have the ear of one or two members of the Magic Council. I could put in a good word for you."

I sighed. This clearly wasn't the first time Ursa had blackmailed someone. I had to do this, or she would land me in a world of trouble. And, as Nugget said, they're just dumb dolls.

"I'll do what I can," I said. "Let's start by you telling me what's been going on in this room."

Ursa did a slow turn, looking around the room. "Normally, my dolls are happy to see me. I spend hours with them, changing their clothes and making sure all their needs are met. But in the last two days, every time I've been in here, I've had an... accident."

"What kind of accident?"

"I've tripped over, and things have been thrown at me. I've even been cut." She pulled up her sleeve. Her arm was covered in what looked like small cat scratches.

"The dolls did this to you?"

She pushed down her sleeve, and lifted her chin. "Yes. I fell over something and several of them jumped on me. I don't think they meant any harm, but they got a bit rough. They were very playful."

"Those marks on your arm show they meant you harm. You shouldn't come in here if it's not safe."

"It's safe. Or it will be once you get rid of the ghost messing with them. That has to be what this is. An evil entity is possessing these dolls and making them do things they'd never normally dream of."

I looked around. Although none of the dolls' expressions were happy, I sensed nothing too dark in here. I went to touch a doll.

"Wait!" Ursa tossed a pair of white cotton gloves at me. "Put these on. Remember, finger grease is a bad thing. And don't touch any of the dolls on the right-hand side of the room. They're the most valuable."

I put on the gloves, then walked around the room. I picked up a couple of dolls and turned them over under Ursa's glare.

I wasn't sensing anything like I'd experienced in Luna's apartment. This must be a different ghost. Or maybe not a ghost at all. Or the dolls had just gotten bored with Ursa and wanted to escape her suffocating mothering behavior.

A loud, low clanging noise made me jump. "What was that?"

"Just the doorbell. Whatever's the matter with you?" Ursa walked to the window. "Oh. We may have a small problem."

"Who is it?" I hurried over to join her.

"Your friend, Olympus Duke, is outside."

I stared down at him. He had a ball of light glowing over his head and was peering through the window on the ground floor.

"What's he doing here?" I turned to Ursa. "Did you contact the Magic Council without telling me? Is this a set up?"

"Of course I didn't. You agreed to help me with my problem. I always keep my word."

I wasn't certain if Ursa was telling the truth. "Do you think he's following me? He saw us coming here and wondered what I was up to."

"His visit probably has nothing to do with you. Stay here. I'll get rid of him." Ursa marched out of the room, slammed the door shut, and locked it.

I raced to the door and tried the handle. There was no way I wanted to be locked in with all these creepy dolls, but the door wouldn't budge.

I turned slowly and plastered my back against the door. Death by deranged doll wasn't how I wanted to die.

Nugget mooched around the room, sniffing several dolls. He knocked a few down with his paw.

"Don't annoy them," I said. "There are way too many of them to take on at once if they turn nasty."

"They don't bother me," Nugget said. He squeaked as a blonde-haired doll dropped off the top shelf and landed on his back. It wrapped its arms around his neck.

"Hey! Hands off my cat." I hurried over and grabbed the doll. She turned her head and hissed at me.

I staggered forward as I was whacked on the back as more dolls descended on top of us. They slammed into me with their hard little heads and fists.

Something cold and sharp jabbed into the back of my hand.

"We're under attack! Russell, take down any dolls attacking from above. Hilda, I need you to stomp on the enemy." I placed her on the floor, touched her back, and stepped away as she grew into a huge, magnificent, hairy spider with giant fangs to match.

She nodded at me and then slashed her limbs through the mass of dolls descending upon us.

"Nugget, destroy everything that moves," I yelled.

A blast of orange magic shot out of him, and a dozen dolls exploded.

I ducked to avoid being sliced to death by the porcelain sailing through the air.

I stumbled back and tumbled over a mass of waiting dolls behind me. They jumped on me as I hit the floor and stabbed me with their little hands, the air full of hisses and tiny screams of anger.

Above the noise of the fury-filled dolls, there was a high-pitched squeaky sound.

I peered at the shelves to see one doll sitting on a small gold throne, with several other dolls surrounding her like they were her personal guards. She was pointing at the others and babbling so fast I couldn't make sense of her words. It looked like she was in charge of this attack.

I yanked several dolls off my head, losing hair as I did so. I rolled onto my hands and knees, grabbed a doll and slung it at the door, just as it opened.

The doll smashed into Ursa's chest and dropped to the floor in pieces.

Ursa blinked rapidly as she bent and picked up the ruined doll. She pressed her lips together as she took in the carnage in the room.

"Before you turn me over to the Magic Council for destroying your dolls, they attacked first." I pulled a doll off my arm and dropped it to the floor.

Ursa's cheeks flushed bright red and her jaw trembled. "You've... you've ruined my collection. My beautiful dolls. You're a monster."

"It was ruin them or be killed." I extracted Nugget from a pile of dolls and held him in my arms. "Where's Olympus? You didn't invite him in, did you?"

Ursa simply stared at me, horror written all over her face.

"Ursa! Where is Olympus?"

She swallowed. "I... I sent him away. I brought you here to help me."

Russell squawked and settled on my shoulder, and Hilda scuttled over. I touched her back, and she shrank to her normal size.

"My collection." Ursa staggered into the room and sank to her knees. "This was my life's work, and you've destroyed it in only a few minutes."

"What was I supposed to do?" I said. "Let the dolls take me and my familiars out? They wanted blood. Some of them got it." My hands were covered in small, stinging cuts.

"My dolls are worth more than the life of a single, damaged witch." Ursa crawled around, collecting pieces of dolls and setting the ones that weren't too damaged back on the shelves.

"Don't get too close to that one in the middle. The doll on the throne," I said. "I've been watching her. I think she's the source of your problems."

Ursa stopped in front of the doll who now looked like a picture of wide-eyed dolly innocence. "It can't be Mary-Sue. She's such a good girl. She always sets an excellent example for the other dolls."

"I'm telling you, Mary-Sue may look like a sweetheart, but that doll has a heart of evil. Get rid of her, and your problems will be over."

Chapter 4

"I made a mistake coming to you for help." Ursa shook her head, her attention on her precious dolls.

I tried to help her pick up bits of smashed up doll, but she pushed me away. "Just go. You've done enough damage. I'll have to figure out another way to deal with this ghost. I should have known better than to waste my time giving you a chance to prove yourself."

I stopped grabbing up pieces of doll and looked around the room. "Ursa, I don't think this is a ghost problem. I'm not the best witch to help you if this is something more complicated, like a curse or a hex."

"You're right about that. You're the worst witch," she muttered.

"Then why come to me for help? It can't just be because I see ghosts easily. Lots of magic users have that ability."

Ursa sat back on her heels and sighed. "It was because of your connection with Magda. I gave you the benefit of the doubt. I wanted to see if you could still be useful to Witch Haven. Useful to me. Instead, you abused my hospitality and destroyed my precious doll collection. And now you accuse

Mary-Sue, one of my most beloved dolls, of being the leader of these atrocities."

I looked over her shoulder and my eyes widened. "Um... Ursa, you need to pay closer attention to Mary-Sue."

The doll was slowly rising from the shelf, her arms outstretched and her teeth bared.

"Was this just a game to you?" Ursa gestured at her ruined collection. "You're mocking me because of my interests? I know people think I'm old-fashioned and set in my ways, but why shouldn't I have a hobby I enjoy? My dolls bring me comfort. Mary-Sue is no exception. I refuse to believe she's involved in this. You're behind this."

"No, I'm not. And you need to take a look for yourself. Mary-Sue's about to pounce on you."

Ursa pointed at the door. "Get out! Take your familiars and your lies and leave my house. I never want to see you again. In fact, leave Witch Haven. No one wants you here. And once I'm through with you, everyone will know you deceived the Magic Council. And I expect you were involved with what happened to Luna. You're just a spoiled witch."

I looked at the evil expression on Mary-Sue's face, and then at Ursa as she continued to rant at me. Since I couldn't convince her of her doll's unstable behavior, Ursa would have to experience what was about to happen to her. Maybe it would make her change her mind about me, and she'd stop throwing accusations my way if she had an evil doll stabbing her in the head.

I crossed my arms over my chest and leaned back against the wall.

"And another thing. I'm going to tell everyone—" Ursa shrieked as Mary-Sue jumped and landed on the back of her head.

The doll sank its tiny teeth into Ursa's hair and clung on for dear life.

Ursa bucked and writhed, screaming and hopping around as she tried to dislodge the doll.

"That doesn't look much fun. Should we help her?" Hilda said.

"Mary-Sue or Ursa?" Nugget said.

I stayed where I was as Ursa staggered about. "Not just yet. Sometimes, a person has to experience a difficult challenge before they learn a valuable lesson." I tried not to smile. Anyone who collected this many scary-faced dolls needed a little payback.

"Get it off me!" Ursa blundered over to me and crashed to the floor by my feet. "It's chewing through my hair. It's trying to kill me."

"I'll help, so long as you admit Mary-Sue could be the problem in your house."

"I won't do that. She's an angel."

"Then we should leave you and Mary-Sue to get to know each other better. I hope you survive the night."

"Wait! Don't go. Just get it off me, please."

"Do you now think Mary-Sue may be a little possessed?"

"Yes! Whatever you say." Ursa kept reaching for the doll, but couldn't get a hold of her. "I can't believe I brought a demon doll into my home."

I placed my hands on the back of Mary-Sue, making her hiss at me. "Hold still. If you move, my magic could hit you."

Ursa shook beneath me as I fired up a spell and poured it into the doll.

Mary-Sue screamed, rolled around, and then dropped off Ursa's head. She lay on the floor in a crumpled heap, smoke billowing from her white dress.

Ursa crawled to the door, wrapped her hands around her knees and drew them up to her chest. Her face was pale and sweaty. "Why did she attack me? I've always been good to her."

I stepped on Mary-Sue to make sure she didn't creep off and start plotting her next assault. "How long have you had her?"

Ursa swiped a hand across her sweating forehead. "I got her a month ago. I picked her up from a collector. It was the first time I'd dealt with him. He seemed professional, and his prices were reasonable. I got her for a steal."

"Maybe there's a reason you got Mary-Sue so cheap," I said. "Could this collector have given you a hexed doll? He wanted to offload it because she was causing him too much hassle?"

"No! She has such a sweet face," Ursa said. "And she's been here for weeks. Why would she turn on me now?"

"It could be a latent curse," Hilda said from her position on my shoulder. "Or a hex that needed something to stimulate it."

I nodded. "Maybe the magic contained in the doll is interested in your power. And this house has a unique quality to it. You said yourself there are plenty of ghosts already here. That particular brew could have been what the curse or hex needed. It fired to life, then got Mary-Sue planning murder. And she could have infected the other dolls. That's why they've begun to misbehave."

Ursa raised a shaking hand and pointed a finger at me. "No! This is because of you. You ruined my dolls, just like you ruined Witch Haven."

Now she was getting mean, and after I saved her from Little Miss Kill-A-Lot. "I had nothing to do with your dolls getting spiteful. This is the first time I've seen them. How would I have managed to hex Mary-Sue and then made sure you bought her? I didn't even know you collected dolls until I came face-to-face with this porcelain nightmare."

"I'm not talking about my dolls." Ursa rested her head back against the wall. "Something... dark seeped into this village after you and Magda were taken away."

It wasn't the first time someone had mentioned this. I leaned back against the wall. "Do you know that for sure, or are you guessing?"

"Everyone felt it. The day you and Magda turned dark, the atmosphere in the village changed."

"Because of the killings." I swallowed down my guilt. "A horrible event like that changes a place forever."

"Not just because of the killings, although they were awful. It was as if a spiteful mist descended on the village. People changed. This used to be a friendly place, neighbors talked to each other and checked in on each other. Now, people keep out of each other's way. They have no time to spend being nice." Her gaze shot to me, and fear flashed across her face. "What darkness did you leave behind?"

I closed my eyes for a second and rubbed my forehead as a cloak of sadness settled over me. "To my knowledge, I left nothing behind. And I was telling you the truth about what I found in Magda's journals. There was a dark witch coven wanting to take over the village. If we hadn't been stopped that day, this place would be entirely different. I'm so sorry for what happened. I wish I could go back and change it. And if what we did changed the fabric of the village, I also regret that."

"Your regret is worthless now."

I looked around the messed up room. "Maybe this killer doll situation has nothing to do with that. But..." I needed someone to confide in about my situation, but Ursa was the wrong person. She'd always been sneaky, and I just didn't trust her.

"But what?" Ursa said. "What do you know? Can you change things? Are you a part of this dark coven, and you're back to finish what you started?"

I shook my head. "I know as much as you, but I want to find out more. Tell me about this darkness. When I asked about any problems in the village at Magda's house, you said there was nothing wrong. Why hide that?"

"Because this is my home, and I want to remember it how it used to be." Ursa's glare softened. "It isn't the same, and it's getting worse. Your friend was taken, and now my dolls have turned into tiny killers with an attitude problem."

"What else?" Was this doll possession a part of something bigger?

Ursa stared at the smoldering remains of Mary-Sue pinned under my boot. "Unexpected fires breaking out in people's houses, animals behaving strangely, spells misfiring, and then the ghosts playing up. And my gnomes... they've been chanting late at night. They won't tell me what's wrong, but I sense they are also unsettled."

I nodded. When you add that all together, there was a much bigger problem going on in Witch Haven. Something dark was brewing in this village, and I had to stop it before it wiped everyone out.

I looked at the mess I'd made. "I'm sorry about your doll collection. I didn't mean to damage them. I really was trying to help."

Ursa's bottom lip jutted out. "If Mary-Sue hadn't jumped on me, I wouldn't have believed it. But I see now that my dolls are dangerous. I'll seal this room until the problem can be resolved."

"And I'll help if I can, although I'm not sure what I can do. Hexes and curses aren't my speciality. And my magic isn't working quite right."

"No, you've done enough. I should have believed you when you said you couldn't help me. I'll find another way."

"If I can't help you, maybe you can help me to uncover this mystery in the village. All the things you told me about, they could be connected. And it's more evidence to show the Magic Council. They may listen if other people are also having troubles. Some of these problems must have been reported to them."

"I'm sure they have been." Ursa pulled herself upright and smoothed down her dress. "But the Magic Council has bigger things on their mind. You're a problem for them, and until they've dealt with you, they won't be interested in reports of dogs going into the cemetery and digging up their masters, or a misbehaving collection of dolls trying to kill their owner."

"They should be interested. If they're not, then they're missing the bigger picture. You know people on the Magic Council. Talk to them. See if you can get them to put the pieces together."

She shook her head. "It hardly seems fair to exploit my resources, given what you've done to my dolls."

"Your dolls are murderous nightmares. You should sling them on a bonfire and incinerate them."

Her eyes narrowed. "It's time you left. And don't come back."

I stood my ground. If I could get Ursa on side, she'd be a powerful ally. The Magic Council wouldn't ignore her pleas for help. "You need to speak up about these problems. If no one is talking about them, how will the Magic Council ever help?"

"They'll help once you turn yourself in. They'll deal with you and then pay attention to the other problems." Ursa jabbed a finger at me. "I'm still not convinced you're innocent. And you've been in my house for less than an hour, and it's in tatters. I dread to think what will happen once you've been in the village for a couple of months."

"Nothing will happen. I may even make this place better if people don't stand in my way." Was Ursa being spiteful, or was she born this way?

Ursa stood back and gestured at the door.

I could have continued arguing with her, but there was zero point. Once a bad witch, always a bad witch, that's how she saw me.

With a heavy heart and dragging feet, I left the room. I trudged down the stairs with my familiars and out the front door. It slammed behind me.

"Don't listen to Ursa," Hilda said. "She was only saying those things because you upset her. She seems to care more about those dolls than people."

"Some of what Ursa said was true, though. The Magic Council is focused on me. If they continue to believe I'm the source of all this trouble, then they won't look anywhere else."

"Then we'll make them look. We'll show them evidence and prove you have nothing to do with this and you're trying to help," Hilda said.

"If we're going to face the Magic Council, we'll need backup," Nugget said. "We're awesome, and can always help you take down a bunch of killer dolls, but you need more witch power on your side."

I nodded. "I'll speak to Odessa and Storm tomorrow. They may help. But I don't want to drag them into the middle of my mess and get them in trouble."

"They're your friends, they won't mind," Hilda said. "And you know they want to find out what happened to Luna as much as you do."

I huffed out a breath. During my time away from Witch Haven, I'd gotten used to ignoring offers of help, and had shut myself away so I didn't see anyone and only had myself to rely on. It still felt alien to hold out a hand when I was in need. But Storm Winter and Odessa Grimsbane were two of my oldest friends. Alongside them and Luna, I had a great set of girl pals when growing up. And I knew I could rely on them now.

Fortified by my decision, I increased my pace, eager to get away from Gravesend Manor and Ursa's harpy behavior and her freaky dolls.

I'd just reached the gate and was struggling to get it open, when someone grabbed me from behind.

"At last. I knew if I waited long enough, I'd get you!"

Chapter 5

I screamed, grabbed the arm of whoever was attacking me, and blasted them with a zinger of a spell.

There was a very male sounding grunt from behind me, but whoever it was held on tight.

I kicked back, hoping to hit a bony bit, while Russell zoomed overhead, squawking and flying down to attack my unknown assailant.

Nugget stared behind me, his eyes widening as his fur puffed out.

"Do something!" I yelled at him.

Nugget shook his head. "I don't want to get arrested."

Arrested? I raised another spell and sparked it on my fingers. "That first hit was a warning. The next time, I shoot to kill."

"How very like you, Indigo Ash."

I froze. I recognized that voice now I'd processed it. Worst nightmare come true. It was Olympus Duke.

I reined in my spell and stopped struggling. "How did you know I was here?"

His grip eased a fraction, but he didn't let me go. "I knew you'd come out of hiding, eventually."

Russell swooped down again, aiming his talons at Olympus.

"Call off your familiars, or I'll arrest them, too," he said.

I squeezed my eyes shut for a second. I didn't want any of my familiars to get injured or in trouble for defending me against Olympus. "Back off, everyone."

Russell flapped to the top of the iron gates and sat on them, cawing angrily.

I couldn't see where Hilda had gone, but she'd been dislodged from my shoulder when Olympus grabbed me. I hoped she wasn't hurt.

"Are you going to let go of me, or is this your attempt at a slow dance?" I asked.

"That depends. Will you run if I let you go?"

There was no point in making a run for it. As Head of the Magic Council, Olympus had advanced magic using abilities, and all the permits needed to blast it at me with no repercussions.

It caused me pain to concede to him, but I nodded. "I won't run."

He released me and stepped back. I turned to face him and winced at his angry expression. Blood dripped down one cheek. It looked like Russell had gotten in a few good strikes before I'd called him off.

"So, what have I done wrong this time?" I tilted my head and placed my hands on my hips.

"All of you are in trouble," Olympus said. "I know your familiars helped get you out of the room I had you held in."

"Have you any proof of that?" Not so many days ago, Nugget, Hilda, and Russell performed an awesome jailbreak. They got me out of a magically warded room, free from the building, and away from the clutches of the Magic Council, before they stripped me of my powers.

"They're your familiars. That's what they're here for, to do your bidding. And they have to pay for their crimes."

Nugget snorted. "I do no one's bidding. I'm not a slave. I choose to be with Indigo. I can leave anytime I want to."

"It's true. Nugget is his own cat," I said. "Just like Hilda is her own spider, and Russell, well, you get the idea. They don't deserve to be punished for anything. I broke out on my own."

"That's impossible. Your magic was impaired at the time." Olympus' dark gaze ran over me. "Although I see that's changed. What did you do?"

My hand went to the necklace I wore. "I stopped doubting myself. My magic came back when I needed it the most."

"A likely story. Not that it matters where you got that extra magic from." Olympus' stern expression hardened. "I had an unhappy Judge Zimmerman visit Witch Haven to conduct your hearing. He was displeased to learn you'd escaped my custody."

"I'm sure the judge understood. An innocent witch must look after herself. He wouldn't want a grave injustice on his hands. That wouldn't do his judgely reputation any good."

Olympus narrowed his eyes. "He raged at me for over an hour. He suggested I was incompetent."

"Then he knows you well," Nugget said.

"Hush. That's no way to talk to an esteemed member of the Magic Council." I repressed a grin. I wasn't getting out of this, so I may as well have fun with Olympus before he arrested me and inflicted some cruel punishment.

"He'll be back. Especially once I've secured you again. And this time, you'll be under guard. I won't let you out of my sight."

"You poor thing. That won't be any fun for you," I said. "All I'll be doing is napping and enjoying all the snacks you bring me. There will be snacks, won't there? A prisoner has rights."

His expression hardened. "Ensuring a dangerous witch is finally imprisoned for the rest of her life will be my fun."

I held up a hand. "Just before you take away my freedom and ruin my life, how did you know I was here? Are you tracking me?"

"No, I'm not tracking you. Did you get the note I left at your house?" Olympus said.

"I did. But why did you think I'd go back to Magda's house? There's nothing there for me. Not after you ordered your goons to destroy it." I swallowed my panic. Did he know I was hiding the house, or was he working on an unfounded hunch that a little magic was in play?

Olympus breathed in deeply. "I knew you wouldn't be able to resist going back to take one last look at the place you called home. I wanted to give you a final chance to turn yourself in. Giving yourself up would be looked on more favorably than if you're arrested. But it's too late for that now."

"Okay, well deduced. But how did you know I was visiting Ursa?"

He lifted one shoulder. "I didn't. That was just fate stepping in to help me out. When Ursa answered the door, she told me you invaded her home. She said she was scared for her life."

"I knew we couldn't trust her," Nugget said. "I hope all the dolls turn on her and attack her in her sleep."

I repressed a smile. I also secretly hoped the dolls would get revenge on my behalf. I'd been doing Ursa a favor by facing off with her hexed horrors, and this was how she repaid me.

"Dolls?" Olympus said.

"It's another story. Although... it could all be linked to something bigger."

He arched a brow. "Bigger than a dark witch trying to finish what she started?"

I pursed my lips. This conversation had to go well, or I was in a world of trouble.

"Let's move," Olympus said. "I need to get you processed and somewhere secure before you cause any more damage."

"I was being helpful to Ursa. These days, I'm a reformed character. Ursa has a hexed house problem. Or possibly a ghost, but I don't think it's your standard haunting."

He sighed. "She always has some problem or other. That's just in her nature."

"It sounds like you're not much of an Ursa fan either."

"I can't comment on that. Let's go."

"Hear me out before I lose my liberty. It'll only take a few minutes, and then I won't say another word."

"You'll need to say a few words when you confess to your crimes."

Olympus was like a dog with his favorite bone when it came to seeing wickedness in me, he just wouldn't let it go.

"I think there's a bigger problem in Witch Haven. The Magic Council has missed it," I said.

"We miss nothing. And we're in full control of the situation now we have you."

"I'm not your biggest problem. And you'll soon see that once you arrest me." I backed away as Olympus beckoned me closer. "Don't try telling me this place has been trouble-free since I was arrested. If you do, I'll know you're lying."

"It hasn't been idyllic. There will always be a few unstable magic users to keep an eye on, but nothing like you."

"Have you seen an increase in magic-related problems in Witch Haven over the last decade?"

He leaned back on his heels. "If we have, it's under control. And we don't want it getting worse because you've moved back."

"I think it will get worse, but it won't have anything to do with me. Luna's haunted apartment, Ursa's hexed manor house, and all the weird happenings in the area, they're connected. And they're a small part of something much bigger. A darkness has entered the village, and it'll only get worse unless we tackle it."

"We're not tackling anything. You're a criminal. You're a part of the problem."

"But you admit there is a problem? How bad have things got?"

"Indigo, you're only making this worse for yourself by resisting arrest."

"I've resisted nothing. I'm interested in the place I live in." And I hadn't resisted, not yet. But I had to get Olympus to listen to me.

He shrugged. "Hauntings and strange goings-on aren't unusual in Witch Haven. After all, this is a center for magic."

"Sure, but I'm only interested in the problematic magic, or troublesome hauntings."

He stared at me. "Perhaps there has been a slight shift in paranormal activity and misfiring magic. Occasionally, a ghost needs re-education, just like some witches do. But as I said, everything's under control."

"So where is Luna? Why haven't you found her? If you have a handle on the darkness ruining this place, bring her back."

"There's no case to investigate. Her uncle has no proof Luna was taken from the hospital. She could have checked herself out and gone on a vacation."

"Olympus! That's bull-hang! Her room was messed up. And she was still weak from being drained by that ghost. Luna wouldn't have had the energy to go anywhere. Have you even tried to locate her?"

He pulled back his shoulders, and his scowl deepened. "No formal investigation has been launched. Besides, you're my focus."

"I shouldn't be. It means you're missing what else is going on. Ursa told me about the magic misfiring, things being set alight, and animals behaving strangely. That's all normal?"

"In a village filled with magic users, it's not unusual."

"You're wrong. Witch Haven isn't safe anymore."

"I agree. It isn't safe whilst you're in it."

"No, not me. How many times do I have to say this? And I have proof that Magda was influenced by a witch coven. They made her attack the other villagers."

"What kind of proof?"

"I found some of Magda's journals. She left me a message telling me she wasn't responsible for what happened."

"Of course, she'd say that. A dark witch will absolve herself of her wrongdoings in an attempt to get away with her misdeeds."

"No! Magda was exploited by this coven. They took personal items of mine and threatened my life if she didn't do what they wanted her to."

"If this is true, why didn't she come to us and get help?"

"Because she was scared for my life. They would have killed me. And the witch she was dealing with lied to her. She said they wouldn't harm any villagers, and the magic was only meant to control and subdue. Magda would never have used it if she knew it could kill."

"That's not proof. It's just her words. And they mean nothing," Olympus said.

My rising anger and frustration made magic spark on my fingers. I clenched my hands behind my back to stop Olympus seeing. "You knew Magda. You've even told me you thought her behavior was odd. This explains it. And she hid the information using magic inside her journal so I'd find it. There was no point in doing that. If she'd wanted other people to know, she'd have written it for anyone to see. Or Magda could have told you what happened after she'd been arrested."

Olympus was quiet for several seconds. Maybe I was getting through to him. He had to have a heart beating inside that broad chest of his.

"Magda always was a decent witch, until the end," he said. "I've always been puzzled as to what made her go bad."

"The dark witch coven happened. They threatened my life, and she acted to protect me. She thought she could control the magic, but it was too much for her."

"Even if I believe that, why did you act the way you did? What caused you to turn on the village?"

"That was never the plan, but the magic she'd been given was too strong for her to contain and it seeped out. I became infected. And it messed with my memories. All I know is that I began to have dark thoughts about everyone, and would talk to Magda about what we could do about the Witch Haven problem. Neither of us was in control."

He rubbed the back of his neck. "Do you still have this journal entry?"

"Of course. And I can show it to you. It's at the—" I stopped myself from saying the house. As far as Olympus knew, Magda's house no longer existed. "It's in safe keeping. I can bring it to you."

He worked his jaw from side to side. "It's a good story, and it even gives me pause, but the issues in Witch Haven are to do with you and Magda."

I shook my head and sighed. He hadn't listened to a word I'd said. I understood his caution, but he was so closed-minded. That's what years of leading a bureaucracy does to you. You lose touch with the real world. I'd never get through to him if he kept this attitude in place.

"I've heard enough, Indigo. Come with me. Then you can tell me where this journal is. I'll take a look and draw my own conclusions."

There was no way I was telling Olympus about Magda's house. If he didn't already have enough suspicions about me, he would once he knew my familiars had concealed the house to stop it being destroyed, and we were secretly living there.

So, I did what every witch would do when her back was against the wall. I cast a look around to make sure my familiars were okay. Hilda had joined Russell on the gate, and Nugget was licking his paw.

I sparked up a spell.

"Don't do anything foolish." Olympus raised a hand.

I blasted the spell at his chest.

He reeled back, letting out a yelp as my knockback spell hit home.

"Run!" I turned to the gate, yanked it open, and we raced away from Ursa's manor house.

Hilda launched herself at me and clambered onto my shoulder. "Oooh! You shouldn't have done that. You'll be in so much trouble."

"You heard him! He didn't believe me. So much for getting Olympus Duke on our side. He thinks the problems in Witch Haven have to do with me."

"Well... they did get worse after you and Magda blasted the place to pieces and killed all those people. He's got every right to be suspicious of you." Nugget cantered along beside me.

"Hey! You're supposed to be on my side." I checked over my shoulder. Olympus wasn't following yet, but he wouldn't be far behind.

"What do we do now?" Hilda said. "I still think we can find a way to bring him around. You could send him a copy of Magda's journal entry with the details of how the witch coven tricked her. He already has his doubts about what happened that day. That could persuade him to go easy on you after the whole hitting him with a spell business back there."

"It's too late for that. We have to do this without him. We'll go back to the house, hide out, and come up with a plan. And first thing tomorrow, we'll—" my breath whooshed out of me as I was taken off my feet by three scarecrows with glowing eyes and scary smiles painted on their faces.

Russell squawked as he flew over our heads.

"Scarecrows! Run!" Nugget yelled.

"No! Don't run. Help me." I lost sight of my familiars as the scarecrows thrust a bag over my head and dragged me away.

"Ouch! Wait! What are you doing? Are you Odessa's scarecrows? We're friends."

I grunted as something hard hit the side of my head, and the fight drained out of me as I blacked out.

Chapter 6

It felt like I was being stabbed with lots of small scratchy pins. They dug into my arms, legs, and the side of my face.

I opened one eye and looked around. I was in a hay barn. At least, it looked like a hay barn. I was surrounded by bales of hay, and there was a rough, bare wood ceiling overhead.

I rolled onto my back and winced as my head protested. Those scarecrows had hit me hard.

I had no idea how long I'd been out for, but there was a pale dawn-like light filtering in through the warped boards, suggesting it had been hours.

"She's finally back with us." Odessa Grimsbane appeared at the top of a ladder, a smile on her round face. "We thought you'd never wake up."

"Did you set those scarecrows on me?" I eased myself up gingerly and tensed, half expecting the scarecrows to be waiting to launch another attack.

Odessa climbed the rest of the way up the ladder and eased herself onto the hay beside me, smoothing her hands over her pumpkin colored tunic. "Noooo! That wasn't my doing. I'd never send attack scarecrows after you."

"Then who sent them? You're the queen of the scarecrows around here."

She twirled a piece of hay between her fingers. "I've been having one or two problems with my scarecrows lately. Well, I say lately. Ever since you and Magda unleashed a darkness onto the village, they haven't been themselves. They're prone to bursts of anger and enjoy misbehaving at every opportunity. I've even had to send some away to advanced training school to see if I can get them to behave."

"There's an advanced training school for scarecrows?"

"Oh, yes! I was mentored by September O'Dell. He's excellent at dealing with the problem children. It's important you make scary scarecrows. But if they get too scary, everyone runs away in terror when they see them, and not just the crows."

"Hmmm, I'm not sure I can take the blame for your scarecrows going haywire. Although it seems I'm being blamed for everything that's going wrong in this village."

"I don't blame you for anything." She smiled brightly. "Who else is pointing the finger at you?"

"Olympus Duke, for one."

"Oh, ignore Limpy. He gets so serious about his work. Which reminds me, I must send him a hamper of pumpkin goodies. He's always more cheerful when he gets a treat from my farm."

Storm Winter's head appeared at the top of the ladder. "At last. Odessa wouldn't let me have any of her pumpkin muffins until you woke up."

"There are pumpkin muffins?" My stomach grumbled at the prospect of something delicious baked by Odessa.

"Of course. Always." Odessa rubbed her hands together. "And not only that, I've got pumpkin spiced lattes and pumpkin and chocolate chip pancakes. As always, we have a glut of pumpkins on the farm, so I need to find inventive ways to use them up. Are you feeling up to something to eat?" She gently stroked my forehead.

"I'm always ready for your pumpkin muffins." Odessa ran a successful pumpkin farm and a scarecrow manufacturing business. The two went hand-in-hand, since scarecrows needed heads and large pumpkins were perfectly head-shaped. Well, they were if you were a scarecrow.

"Storm, bring up the goodies. We can eat up here while we catch up. I'm dying to know why my scarecrows brought you down. You must have been doing something to make them unhappy."

"Um... not that I know of. They just jumped me. What time is it?" I said.

"Just after five in the morning. I'm up before dawn at the moment, scarecrow wrangling. My straw-filled wonders are keeping me on my toes," Odessa said. "Anyway, enough about my scarecrows—"

"Before we move on from your terrifying scarecrows, where are the three that attacked me?"

"Don't worry about them. They're safely back in their barn. They slipped their chains and escaped. One of them told me you were running away from

Ursa Wyrm's house. I didn't know you two were friends."

"We're not." I looked around. "Where are my familiars?"

"I sent them home. They followed the scarecrows here. They were worried about you, but I said we'd take care of you." Odessa leaned closer. "Now, tell me everything about Ursa. What have you been up to?"

I removed a piece of hay sticking into my side and flicked it away. "Ursa's not a friend, that's for sure. And we're definitely more enemies after last night. I almost got caught by Olympus Duke because Ursa informed on me."

"Ursa's such a sneak." Storm heaved a huge hamper onto the hay and joined us. "But what were you doing at her house?"

"Being mildly blackmailed into looking at her haunting problem. Or should I say, her creepy killer hexed doll problem. Ursa bought a rogue doll off a dodgy collector, and it's been wreaking havoc ever since."

"Ursa blackmailed you?" Odessa flipped open the lid of the wicker hamper. She handed around enormous caramel frosted pumpkin muffins and travel mugs of steaming latte.

I nodded, but no one spoke for several seconds as we all enjoyed the muffins and hot drinks.

I swallowed my huge mouthful and licked sugar off my lips. "According to Ursa, she used to combine magic with Magda."

Odessa nodded. "I remember that."

"I don't. Anyway, Ursa caught Nugget poking around her yard, and brought him back to Magda's house."

"The house that's supposed to be hidden?" Storm said.

"Yep. She sensed the magical wards and broke through them. Ursa said if I didn't help her with her problem, she'd tell the Magic Council where I was."

Odessa shook her head, while Storm's top lip curled.

"I shouldn't have bothered helping because she did it, anyway. And now Olympus knows I'm still in the area. And..." I paused for another bite of delicious muffin.

"It gets worse?" Storm said.

"It does. Olympus was going to arrest me. I tried to reason with him, but he wouldn't see sense, so... I blasted him in the chest with a spell and ran off."

Odessa bit her bottom lip. "Oh, Indigo. That's bad."

"It wasn't my most mature move, but it was my only move at the time. He had me cornered. It was either that or go back to prison. And until the Magic Council see sense about what happened to Magda, and I figure out where Luna is, I'm not going back behind bars."

"You'll never go back behind bars ever again if we have anything to do with it," Odessa said. "It's not fair the way you've been treated. I love having you back in Witch Haven. You belong here. And you're helping. You helped deal with Luna's problem."

"Not really. And about that. We need to talk. I was planning on coming to see you both tomorrow. Well, it's tomorrow now, but you get what I mean."

Odessa grinned. "Then my scarecrows did you a favor when they kidnapped you. And I easily stopped them dismembering you, so everything worked out as it should."

"Dismembering?" My mouth fell open. "That's what they had planned for me?"

Storm shook her head. "It didn't happen. Forget about it. They don't usually go that far."

I rubbed the tender spot on the side of my head. Being a scarecrow's plaything wasn't something I'd want to do anytime soon.

"We've also been discussing the Luna situation," Odessa said, with a nod at Storm. "We've done several location spells, and all we can pick up is a faint echo. It's as if she's here, but not here."

"Or she's a ghost," Storm said darkly.

My gut twisted. "You think she's been killed?"

"No! I'm convinced she's alive," Odessa said. "We can't give up hope. And there are still things we can do to locate her. We just need to work together on this and we'll crack it."

I took a sip of the sugary sweet pumpkin latte. I'd come so far in such a short amount of time since returning to Witch Haven, but still had niggling doubts in the back of my mind that I should never have returned.

What if coming back here had enraged the ghosts, and one of them took its anger out on Luna? And what if what Magda and I did all those years ago had infected the village? By returning, I'd aggravated something dark. Maybe I was behind all these problems. Would it be simpler if I left? Would the darkness retreat if it no longer felt my presence?

"A penny spell for your thoughts," Odessa said. "You look troubled. I know it's worrying that Luna's missing, but we'll find her."

I ate my final bite of muffin. "I hate to agree with the Magic Council, but what if they're right about me? Would it be better if I gave myself up? They could investigate to see if I was the cause of these troubles. If they took all my magic, it may neutralize the problem."

"Or it would leave you as a shadow with no home to call your own," Odessa said. "It's the worst idea I've ever heard."

"So you think I have nothing to do with the darkness creeping through the village?"

"What darkness?" Odessa said, a little too brightly to be genuine.

"One of our friends was being haunted by malevolent ghosts and has vanished, Ursa and her killer dolls are acting up, and she was telling me about other problems in the village. Neither of you mentioned those. And then there are your misbehaving scarecrows to add to the list. Should I go on?"

Storm and Odessa shared a guilty look.

"We didn't mention anything because we didn't want to trouble you," Odessa said. "You're still finding your feet. Adding to your worries may change your mind about staying. And I don't want you going anywhere."

"And even if you are the problem," Storm said, "now you're back, you can fix everything."

I wrinkled my nose. Could I? When I'd unleashed darkness on the village with Magda, I hadn't even been aware of what I was doing. How could I undo a problem I didn't even know I'd made?

"Besides, you can't leave. It's not possible," Odessa said.

"Why isn't it possible?"

"We've been out and about, and the Magic Council has patrols at the village exits. It's not hard to figure out who they're on the lookout for," Storm said.

"All this trouble, just to catch me." I shrugged. I really didn't want to leave, so this was the excuse I needed to stick around. "Then it looks like I'm staying."

Odessa clapped her hands. "Yay! That's the right decision."

"We've also been hearing bad things about you from anyone Ursa's spoken to," Storm said. "She's been busy telling everyone you turned her dolls into monsters."

"She's the only monster around here," I said. "And that only happened yesterday evening. How come everyone already knows about it?"

"News travels fast around here. I bet she was gossiping with her neighbors before you'd even whacked Limpy with that spell. And it's just another reason you have to stay, to make sure people don't believe any of these nasty rumors," Odessa said.

I narrowed my eyes, but nodded. It wasn't fair what Ursa was doing. I already had a lousy reputation in the village, and she was making it worse.

"Then I'm definitely not leaving," I said.

"Which we all agree is the best idea." Odessa tapped my knee and handed me a still warm pumpkin and chocolate chip pancake. "I'm not having another friend disappearing. It's bad enough Luna's gone. And to make it worse, her poor uncle isn't keeping up with the orders at the bakery, so I've missed out on my fresh cream cakes."

"Surely you have enough treats to keep you going here," I said around a mouthful of delicious, sweet pancake.

"I'm just an amateur when it comes to cake making. You can't beat someone else's baking," Odessa said. "And Albert's baking is literally magical. But he's so stressed about what's going on with Luna, he keeps forgetting to open on time. When I went in yesterday, several people were complaining about missing orders and late deliveries. With all the stress and worry, he may close the bakery altogether. He relies heavily on Luna, even though there were times when her baked goods were less than perfect."

"She mentioned to me that she had trouble with her baking," I said. "I figured that kind of magic would run in her blood. She has the gift, the same as the rest of her family."

Odessa shook her head. "You would think that, and sometimes, her cakes were out of this world. But Luna was never consistent with what she created. Sometimes, she'd make a fruitcake so sweet and delicious that I could easily eat the whole thing, and then another time she'd present me with a piece that was so hard I almost chipped a tooth."

"Something was going on with her baking magic," Storm said. "I asked her about it after getting sick from eating a cream horn she gave me, but she denied there was a problem."

I finished my pancake and sat back in the pile of hay behind me. "The ghost in her apartment said Luna was keeping secrets. I thought it was blowing hot air at the time to distract me. Was it telling the truth? It would have seen everything going on in her life since it was haunting her. Did Luna have a problem with her magic that she was keeping secret?"

"We'll only learn the answer to that once we've found her," Odessa said.

"And your location spells showed nothing useful?"

Odessa shook her head. "They were unhelpfully vague. I thought I'd mis-cast the magic, but I kept getting the same result."

I nodded. "I did a similar spell, and it didn't help. Hilda thinks Luna is in limbo. Maybe even trapped between worlds."

Odessa's forehead wrinkled. "If that's true, then we have to get her out of there. She'll be so scared."

"Agreed. So what's our next move?" Storm said.

"How about we go back to Luna's apartment?" I said. "There could be clues I missed. The last time I was there, I was focused on getting rid of the ghosts, so I didn't think to look for anything else. If Luna's hiding a secret, that could be the reason she went missing, or even why the ghosts were interested in her in the first place."

"We should go now, before it gets any lighter," Odessa said. "The village is still quiet, so we can sneak in and out without anyone spotting us. And you definitely need to keep a low profile now that Ursa's badmouthing you and the Magic Council is on the hunt for you."

"I will. But Luna has to be our priority. And I just need to keep the Magic Council off my back until we find her and know she's safe."

"And clear your name," Odessa said. "That's important, too."

It was important, but with my best friend in danger, I had to get her back. The rest I'd figure out later.

Storm brushed muffin crumbs off her fingers. "What are we waiting for? Let's go find Luna."

Chapter 7

We headed out of Odessa's hayloft, past a huge field of ripening pumpkins, and then a creepy field full of half-built scarecrows. Most had legs or arms, and all had torsos, but there were only a few with pumpkin heads. They watched us with glowing eyes, a sense of constrained malevolence rippling off their compact bodies.

Odessa sure knew how to make scary scarecrows.

Her farm sat on the outskirts of Witch Haven, but it was only a small village, and we soon reached a more residential area. The lanes were lined with thatched cottages with tiny windows and low doorways a hobbit would feel at home going through.

The cottages quickly gave way to modern buildings, and we turned onto the street Luna's apartment sat on.

I grabbed Storm and Odessa. "Is that someone standing outside her apartment?"

Storm frowned. "We don't need to get any closer to identify that's someone from the Magic Council. Look at the officious way he's standing. And he's wearing one of those dumb hats they always have. They must train them to look that pompous."

"Let's try around the back," Odessa said. "There's an external staircase used for emergencies."

After watching for a few minutes to see if the guard out the front would move on, we tried the back way in. We headed along the deserted alleyway that ran behind the apartments. It housed storage units and the large communal dumpsters used by apartment residents.

Odessa squeaked and shoved me back against the wall so hard my teeth rattled.

"Ouch! What was that for?"

She shooed me away with her hands. "Retreat! There's a guard at the back as well."

"They must really want to catch you," Storm said.

We shuffled behind a dumpster and ducked down.

"There's only one of them," Odessa said after a few seconds of sneaking looks at the guard. "We could use a little diversionary magic on him. Or restrain him so we can get inside."

"We don't want anyone getting hurt," I said.

"Don't you want to help Luna?" Storm said.

"Of course! But... I'm done hurting people with my magic." I chewed on my bottom lip. I really wanted to take a look inside Luna's apartment, and that guard was standing in my way.

"I'll deal with this guy." Storm wiggled her fingers. "I'll distract him while you two get inside."

"What are you going to do to him?" I said.

"Give him something else to think about." She waved us away, and we backed up until we were out of sight of the guard but could still see Storm.

Storm marched over to the guy guarding the door and started talking to him.

"She's not going to hurt him, is she?" I said.

"Oh, no. There won't be any permanent damage. All he'll have is a mild headache," Odessa said. "Maybe some mild short-term memory loss."

"Memory loss!" I made a move to stop Storm, but Odessa grabbed me and shook her head.

"Storm's magic is blunt, but it's effective. Trust her. She knows what she's doing."

I nodded and forced myself not to panic. Storm Winter's name fit her perfectly. Her magic was cold, hard, and could chill a person to the bone if she was in the right mood. Or the wrong mood, depending on which side of the spell you were on.

I chewed on a nail as I waited to see what Storm would do. I almost felt sorry for the guard, but he was stopping us from helping a friend in need, so he had to be removed.

The guard suddenly yelped and slumped to the ground.

Storm turned and gave us a thumbs up, before grabbing him under the armpits and hauling him behind a dumpster.

"Let's move," Odessa said.

We scurried to the back entrance, headed inside, and dashed up the stairs to Luna's apartment, which was on the second floor.

I breathed a sigh of relief when there was no one guarding her actual apartment door. I tried the handle, but it was locked.

"Leave that to me." Glittery magic sparkled out of Odessa's fingers and surrounded the door handle. A second later, the door popped open.

I ducked my head around it and peered inside. "It's all clear."

We headed in, and I took a minute to take in the chaos. It had only been a few days ago that I'd confronted a ghost here, and the damage had yet to be cleared up. There were dried globules of ghost goo on the cream carpet, scorch marks on the walls, and several large indentations in the ceiling.

"I'll search Luna's bedroom," I said. "You take the living room."

Odessa nodded and hurried away.

I headed into Luna's bedroom. It was painted a calming sage green, and if it weren't for the mold flaking off the walls, it would have been a nice place to rest your head.

When we got Luna back, I'd make sure this place looked great before she moved back in. She didn't need any lingering memories of her unhappy time here. She'd loved this apartment until it got taken over by malevolent ghosts.

I searched through her drawers, under her bed, and had a rifle through her closet, but didn't find anything useful. I left the bedroom and headed into the living room.

"Did you find anything?" I asked Odessa.

She was just replacing the cushions on the couch. "Nothing. No deep, dark secrets to put Luna's life in peril. What about you?"

"The same. There were no secrets hanging in the closet. But I've had an idea. How about we try contacting Luna while we're here? She has a strong connection with this place. We could use it as an anchor to draw her close to us if she is in limbo."

"It's worth a shot." Odessa settled on the couch and patted the seat next to her. "Take hold of my hands, we'll see if we can make contact."

I joined her, and we linked hands. "Do you mind leading on the magic? I'm still getting used to my new powers and they sometimes misfire. I don't want this spell to go wrong and blast us into space."

"Space! No, I'm definitely not dressed for space travel. And I don't have my broomstick with me. I'm happy to help," Odessa said. "And I've got something to make the connection stronger." She pulled a small glass bottle from her pocket.

"What is it?"

"It's my speciality ground pumpkin. The energy is concentrated because it's been dried and then ground into a fine powder."

"That sounds... good?"

"It's better than good. This powder strengthens any spell." She patted some onto her palm and did the same to me. "If Luna is out there in limbo, we'll get to her thanks to my pumpkin powered powder."

We held hands again, and I took a deep breath, grounding my magic and focusing on contacting Luna, as Odessa's warm, cinnamon and spice scented magic wound its way around me.

Nothing happened for a few seconds. All I could hear was Odessa softly breathing and kept getting the whiff of pumpkin spice up my nose.

I tilted my head. "Did you hear someone?"

"No. But it could take a while before we find Luna. Give my magic time to work. It's got a lot of places to search."

I squeezed my eyes shut and continued to listen. There it was again. A faint female voice, and she was calling for help.

"Oh! I heard it that time. Do you think that's Luna?" Odessa said.

"It's hard to tell. Someone needs assistance, though. Luna, can you hear me? It's Indigo. I'm in your apartment with Odessa. Do you see us?"

"Help!" The voice was just a whisper in the air. "I'm lost."

"Luna, if you can hear me, say my name. We're trying to find you. We're going to bring you back."

"Help me. It's so dark in here."

"Whoever it is, she sounds scared," Odessa said.

"We're coming for you, Luna. We're looking for you. We won't give up until we get you back." Determination flooded through me. We would get her back. My best friend had to return to Witch Haven. I wasn't letting this ghost win. And Luna going missing was my fault. I'd failed to banish the ghost who'd been hassling her, and now she was in even more trouble.

"Do you know where you are, Luna?" Odessa said.

There was silence.

"I can't hear her anymore," Odessa said. "Has Luna gone?"

"Luna, we're right here in your apartment. Try to find us." My voice wobbled. I desperately wanted her home.

"I'm not sensing anything." Odessa squeezed my hand. "I think she's gone."

I glanced at her, tears making my vision cloudy. "Do you think the ghost took Luna to punish me?"

"No! And I don't think this is about you. Well, not just you. Although I imagine the ghosts were raging mad that you put a stop to their fun."

"Why else would they take Luna if not to get back at me?"

Odessa didn't speak for several seconds. Indecision played across her face before she sighed. "Because of her odd powers."

"You think her dodgy cake baking was the reason she was snatched by the ghosts?"

"It's much more than that. Luna has been hiding something. I've seen her go out at strange hours of the night, yet when I asked her about it, she brushed it off and said she was having trouble sleeping. But I didn't believe her."

"Do you think it's the darkness messing with Luna?" I said.

"I don't know. Maybe. But Luna is such a good witch, that it would take something seriously powerful to push her off her path."

Had I really messed up this entire village? Evil scarecrows, dangerous dolls, toxic hauntings, my best friend turning to dark magic. What next, a plague of frogs descending on us?

Odessa gave me a hug. "Don't get disheartened. Luna made contact with us. That's a great start. She's still alive."

"Maybe we should set up base here. This could be the only place we can make contact with Luna. We could camp out and keep trying to locate her."

"It's too risky to stay. With the Magic Council lurking outside, they'll soon figure out someone is using the apartment. And they'll probably double the guards once they find out what Storm's done." Odessa stood and dusted pumpkin powder off her hands. "Speaking of which, we should get out of here. Storm will only be able to hold that guard for so long. And if he wakes and starts making problems, she might do him serious harm."

"More serious than memory loss?"

Odessa shrugged. "You know Storm. She blasts out magic first and asks questions never."

"Then let's go."

We hurried out of the apartment, back down the stairs, and out into the alleyway.

Storm was leaning against the wall. The guard's boots were sticking out from behind a nearby dumpster.

She straightened when she saw us. "How did it go?"

"We heard her!" Odessa grabbed Storm's hands and swung her arms from side to side. "Luna is still alive. She's scared and lost, but she's still with us."

A rare smile crossed Storm's face. "Did she tell you anything useful?"

"Let's talk more back at my house," I said. "How's the guard doing?"

"He's groaning and about to wake up, so we need to get out of here."

We hurried away, sticking to the back alleys, until we were near my house.

I heaved a sigh of relief as I discovered there were no guards outside, but then there shouldn't be anyone guarding this location. As far as the Magic Council knew, the house had been destroyed. Although I had a bad feeling Olympus knew I was hiding something big here.

I looked around to make sure no one was watching us, then opened a pathway through the magic wards. I sealed it once Odessa and Storm were through, and we hurried into the house.

Nugget was snoozing on his pile of towels in the corner of the living room, Russell was on his perch, and Hilda scurried out from under the magic cabinet.

She scuttled up my leg and onto my shoulder. "We're glad to see you're not dead. When the scarecrows attacked, we thought the worst. We tried to fight them but they were too fast for us to keep up."

"That's all thanks to my powdered pumpkin," Odessa said. "They love it. It gives them a real fire in their straw bellies. Well, not a literal fire. Fire and straw don't mix. But you know what I mean."

"Of course. And the scarecrows kept throwing chunks of raw pumpkin at us," Hilda said. "I almost got flattened by a big jagged piece."

"You didn't get hurt?" I ran my hand carefully over her.

"No, we all kept our distance after that and followed them to Odessa's farm."

"Where I promised you, I'd restore Indigo to perfect health," she said.

My head was pounding, and I still had an egg-shaped lump on my skull, but I nodded. "I'm fine now. And we've been to Luna's apartment to see if we could make contact with her."

"And did you?" Hilda said.

"We did. Although we're still no closer to figuring out where she is. But I have something that could help with that."

"What have you got in mind?" Odessa said.

"It's risky," I said. "It could be dangerous."

"I don't mind risk," Storm said.

Odessa grinned. "Same here. This is exciting."

"Maybe not so exciting. But I think we should talk to the ghost I trapped in Luna's apartment. It could have answers for us about where she is."

"Oooh! Yes, good plan. The ghosts could have been working together. We could do a little ghost interrogation and get it talking," Odessa said.

"I'm always up for some ghost menacing," Storm said. "Especially when they mess with my friends."

"Um, before you do that," Hilda said. "We've got bad news."

"Did something happen while I was away?" I said.

Hilda shuffled her legs. "When we got back to the house, we discovered the ghost jar was missing."

Chapter 8

I raced to the magic cabinet where I'd left the ghost jar and stared at the space it had been sitting in. "How did this happen? Where has it gone?"

"Someone else must know your house is still standing, and they came in and helped themselves to your trapped ghost." Storm joined me, along with Odessa. "Who have you told that this place is hidden behind magic wards?"

"The only people who know are you, Odessa, and my familiars," I said.

"And Ursa," Storm said. "You said she came banging on the front door."

My hands clenched, and I scowled. "She must have seen the ghost jar when she barged in uninvited. But I don't get it. What's she doing sneaking in and taking a trouble making ghost? She's got enough problems with her hexed dolls." I turned to the door, meaning to march out, confront Ursa, and get back what was mine.

Odessa jumped in my way. "Take a breath. It may not have been her."

"It makes sense. She's the only one who knows this place exists apart from everyone in this room. It has to be Ursa."

Odessa raised her hands. "Not necessarily. Maybe someone saw you coming and going and put the pieces together. You wouldn't be visiting this site if there was nothing here but rubble."

What Odessa said made sense, but I was too angry to process everything. I wanted to race back to Ursa's house and make her tell me where she was hiding my ghost.

"And I don't want to give you even more bad news, but Olympus has been snooping around," Hilda said. "Maybe he figured a way through the magic wards, too."

"It can't have been Olympus. The ghost jar was here when we went to Ursa's house, and we left him in her yard, flat on his back after I sprung that spell on him."

"He had time to come back and figure out a way through the magic, and then steal the ghost jar."

"But why would he want it? No, it has to be Ursa. She'll be so sorry for messing with me."

"You're not chasing after her. Not right now," Odessa said. "You need to calm down. If you go after Ursa in the mood you're in, the Magic Council will grab you for sure. You're not thinking clearly."

"Maybe that's what Ursa wants to happen," Storm said. "She's working with the Magic Council to draw you out. She figured you must be keeping that ghost because it's important, so came back and stole it. It's the bait to get you to make a mistake. I bet she's done a deal with the Magic Council and will get a reward once you're arrested."

I gritted my teeth. "It would be such an Ursa thing to do."

Odessa patted my arm. "It was a good idea, thinking we could talk to that ghost, but maybe it wouldn't have helped. Most likely, it would have taunted us and messed us around like it did before."

I rolled my shoulders to loosen the tension in them. It had been a long shot, but I needed something to grab hold of. Something concrete, so I had a way to find Luna. Everything else we tried resulted in dead ends and frustration.

I turned away from the door. "Ursa is welcome to that ghost. She can add it to her creepy collection of misbehaving finds. Maybe it'll get out of the ghost jar and slide into one of her dolls. Then she'll have two murderous dolls on her hands. And she can't blame me for that haunting."

"I'm sure she'll find a way," Storm said.

I would not forget this. Ursa was a snitch and a thief. If she asked for my help again, I'd toss her over my garden fence with a spell that would leave her bruised for days.

"What should we do now we don't have a ghost to question?" Odessa said.

Storm checked her watch. "I know what I need to do. I've got a job I'm running late for. I'll link up with you both tomorrow."

"Is that the puppy job?" Odessa grinned. "I'm so jealous."

"What's a puppy job?" I asked.

"Storm's got a case investigating a missing bundle of cute furriness," Odessa said. "She's getting paid to find fluff balls."

"It's not as much fun as Odessa makes out, but it's not just any missing dog. This is a prize pedigree breeding hellhound. And he's worth a fortune, apparently."

"Someone stole him?" I said.

"Most likely," Storm said. "Puppies sired from this hound fetch a lot of money. There's a waiting list of over two years for one of his pups."

Odessa shook her head. "You must get the fluffy baby back. And if he's sired any pups, return them, too. And any other dogs you find with the people who stole him."

"That's not happening. I'm being paid to find one hellhound. I'm not rescuing a pack."

"Storm! Don't you dare leave a single pup behind, or I'll set my scarecrows on you." Odessa jammed her hands on her hips and glared at Storm until she laughed.

"I'm officially terrified. Fine. I'll bring them all back. But if I can't find the owners, they have to live with you on the farm. Do we have a deal?"

"Of course! I can handle having a few furry babies around until the owners are located. And think how grateful they'll be when you return their fluffy angels to them. You may get reward money."

Storm shook her head, then winked at me. "The owner is paying me a fortune to find this hound, so I can't turn down the job. And I need to meet her to give her an update. But I'll be back to help with Luna as soon as I can."

We said a quick goodbye, and Storm left the room. A few seconds later, she raced back in, alarm written across her face. "We have a problem. Olympus is outside. And he's not on his own."

I groaned as I dashed to the window and peered out. Olympus was looking at the pile of rubble next to the hidden house. He was directing two black-clad members of the Magic Council around as they sifted through the broken bricks.

"He's on to me," I muttered. "You two need to leave before he figures out what's going on."

Odessa shook her head. "We're not leaving you to face the Magic Council on your own."

Storm shrugged. "Indigo can handle them. And I have a hellhound to find. I'll use the back way out of here."

"Storm! We're not leaving Indigo." Odessa gave Storm a hard whack on the arm.

"Creeping broomsticks! She's an Ash witch. She could wiggle her fingers and get rid of that lot with the right spell." Storm rubbed her arm.

"That's not the point. Indigo needs us." Odessa put an arm around my shoulders.

"Thanks for wanting to help, but Storm's right. You both need to go."

"I usually am right." Storm smirked. "And I've really got to go. I can't lose out on this payday."

"Agreed. And I don't want either of you implicated in this mess," I said.

"We're already implicated," Odessa said. "And Luna is our friend, too. We'll have more chance of finding her if we work as a team."

"I'm not saying we can't work on this together, but there won't be any team members left if we're all arrested," I said. "And once the Magic Council know we're working together, they won't look favorably on either of you. Odessa, you could lose business if you're seen associating with me. And Storm, you don't want your PI work to dry up. Potential clients may not trust you if they know we're friends again."

She shrugged. "I've got a great reputation. Hanging out with you won't mess with that. But I need this job so I can get the money. It'll set me right for a couple of months so I can focus on... something else."

I pressed my lips together. Storm hadn't shared with me that her sister, Eden, was missing. Odessa had told me about that tragic event, and that Storm was still focused on finding her, even though Eden had been missing for years.

But it was Storm's secret to tell me when she was ready, and I wasn't standing in her way of helping her family.

I nodded. "I understand. This way. I'll check out back to make sure no one is around. And then you're both leaving." I hurried them to the back door and spent a few seconds checking outside to make sure no sneaky Magic Council members were snooping around.

Once I was certain the way was clear, I gestured for Storm and Odessa to join me. "Head straight to the trees. I'll keep watch to make sure you're not spotted. If you hear anyone yelling, keep going. I'll distract the Magic Council until you get away."

"I'm not sure about this," Odessa said. "I want to stay and help."

I shooed her off the porch. "Go! The longer you linger, the riskier it is for all of us."

"Let's get out of here." Storm grabbed Odessa's arm and dragged her away.

"We'll come post your bail," Odessa said.

Only when I could no longer see them, did I head back inside the house and close the door. I leaned against it and blew out a breath.

I couldn't put this off any longer. I'd been living on borrowed time ever since I'd come back to Witch Haven. It was inevitable that the Magic Council would eventually track me down and confront me.

I had to face them. And when I did, I'd make them hear the truth. There had to be a way through their defences. A way to get them to see I was no longer a bad witch.

I hurried back into the living room, over to the magic cabinet, and pulled out Magda's journal with the hidden entry inside that revealed the dark witch coven. I opened the relevant page and pressed my hand against it. Instantly, the hidden text revealed itself.

It was all I had, but this would have to do. They couldn't all be stuffed shirts at the Magic Council. Someone had to listen to me and consider this new information as important.

"Are you sure about this?" Hilda scuttled up my leg, perched on my shoulder, and tapped her front legs rapidly.

"No, not one tiny bit, but what else can I do? It's do or die time. I've got one shot to make the Magic

Council understand I'm not the biggest threat to this place. And if they keep looking at me as the source of trouble, Witch Haven could be doomed forever."

"So what are you going to do?"

"I'm going outside, and I'm facing my enemy."

Chapter 9

Hilda rode on my shoulder as I walked to the back door. Russell flew next to me, and Nugget strolled along behind us.

I had to face the Magic Council. It looked like Olympus was setting up a permanent watch on this place, and we'd be trapped inside if I didn't move fast. And I only had so many tins of peaches left to sustain me.

Besides, I was done hiding. I would make Olympus listen to me.

"If you fail to convince Olympus not to arrest you, you can always blast him with more magic and make a run for it again," Nugget said. "That sort of worked."

I shook my head. "I'm done running. But I don't want them to know about this house just yet. I'm not losing all of Magda's things. And I'm not losing our home."

"We'll back you up," Hilda said. "Just tell us what you need us to do."

"Hopefully, you won't need to do anything. Try not to get involved. Olympus already thinks you're troublemakers because you helped me bust out of that room."

"Then it won't matter if we get in even more trouble," Hilda said. "Russell and Nugget agree with me."

Russell flapped and cawed, but Nugget simply sat there washing his face.

"Thanks. I appreciate the support. We'll go out the back way. We can make it look like we're approaching the house along the lane. That may throw the Magic Council off the scent, so they stop poking around and don't discover the house." It wasn't a perfect plan, but it may just be enough to stop them.

We snuck out the back door, raced to the trees, and snaked through them. Then we ducked out onto the lane and acted like we were returning from the village.

"There she is!" one of Olympus' companions said. He was a short, skinny guy with flat black hair. "Stop, witch. You're under arrest by orders of the Magic Council. You're charged with—"

"That's enough, Thaddeus," Olympus said. "Indigo knows what she's done."

I lifted my chin. "I do. And I know I'm innocent."

"You deny that you blasted me with magic, before running away when I confronted you at Ursa's house?" Olympus said.

"Oh, well, I'm not innocent of that. I didn't mean that. Besides, that was self-defense." It wasn't, but I'd panicked. "You were trying to arrest me. And you weren't listening to me." I held up Magda's journal.

"I hope you'll give me the opportunity to plead my case now."

"We shouldn't trust her," Thaddeus hissed. "She'll deceive us. She could use her dark magic on us."

"You shouldn't believe all the rumors about me," I said. "I'm not all bad. And neither was Magda."

Olympus glanced at his two colleagues, then nodded at me. "Very well. We'll hear you. But if we don't like what we hear, we're taking you to a full Magic Council meeting. They will decide your fate."

I swallowed. I was taking a huge risk by doing this. "Agreed. This journal contains information about the true dark forces behind the attack on Witch Haven."

"An attack you were heavily involved in," Thaddeus said.

"Let Indigo speak," Olympus said.

"We shouldn't listen to her. We should take her in straightaway," Thaddeus said.

"Who's in charge here?" Olympus said.

Thaddeus instantly backed down. "My apologies. Of course, you know best." From the narrow-eyed look on Thaddeus's face, he was thinking exactly the opposite. It looked like Olympus had a rival.

I paged through the journal until I found the relevant entry. "The problems in Witch Haven began when a coven blackmailed Magda into doing their bidding. They stole personal items of mine and threatened my life. They said they'd kill me if she didn't do what they told her to. They gave her magic, which they claimed would act as a control on the villagers."

"I've never heard such nonsense," Thaddeus said. "Witch Haven is a safe place. Dark magic isn't welcome, and anyone who lives here is protected from such darkness. Or at least they were until you and Magda became so unstable."

Olympus shot Thaddeus an angry look, and he took a step back and muttered an apology.

"That happened because of the witch coven. Magda tried to control the magic they gave her, but it was too strong for her. And it infected me as well. That's why we attacked the villagers. And Witch Haven's problems aren't over yet," I said. "They're going to get much worse."

"They will now you're back," Thaddeus said.

Olympus raised a hand to silence him. "Witch Haven has had more than its fair share of troubles since the darkness descended upon us after that terrible day."

Thaddeus jabbed a finger in my direction. "And here's the reason."

Olympus watched me with a calm expression on his face. I couldn't figure out what he was thinking. "Perhaps Indigo has a point."

I jerked back. Did he believe me?

"The darkness should have receded when the troublemakers were taken away, but things have remained out of balance ever since then," he said.

"Perhaps that's because of so many deaths," his other companion said. He was a short, squat man, dressed entirely in black with a neat goatee.

"I don't disagree with that possibility," I said. "Those deaths opened a path for darkness to creep in. And that's what the witch coven wanted. They needed to create a weakness in the village so it would be easier to take over. They tried to do it using dark magic and Magda, and they failed. Now, they're using this imbalance to make their presence felt. They're destabilizing the goodness in the village to make it easy to take over when they're ready."

"Why wait so long?" Olympus said.

"I... I can't answer that," I said. "Only the coven infecting this place can tell you the reason for the delay."

"Did Magda name the dark witches who troubled her?" Olympus said.

"No, I haven't found any names yet. But I haven't looked through all her journals. I still may find more evidence."

"There isn't any evidence to collect," Thaddeus said. "These are the ramblings of a crazed witch intent on destruction. We shouldn't listen to her."

"Give us a moment, Indigo." Olympus gestured his two colleagues closer, and they conferred quietly for several minutes.

"What do you think?" Hilda whispered in my ear.

"They seem to be listening. Or at least, Olympus is paying attention to what I have to say. That Thaddeus creep definitely isn't."

"I knew Olympus would come round to our way of thinking," Hilda said.

I shifted from foot to foot and held the journal close to my chest. I knew I'd have to pay for my use of illegal magic, attacking Olympus, and lying about what happened to Magda's house, but I could live with that, so long as I got to clear Magda's name.

Olympus turned to us, and my heart sank to my black boots. From the look in his eyes, I'd failed to convince him of anything.

"Indigo Ash, you're under arrest for crimes against magic," he said.

I glanced at my familiars. Nothing I could say would convince Olympus that I was anything other than a broken witch who should be locked away for the rest of her life.

"You're to come with us immediately. There's a full meeting of the Magic Council in progress. They'll determine your sentence. There's no point in dragging this out any longer," he said.

"I... I don't want to be seen by the whole Magic Council. Is that necessary?" I took a step back.

"It is. And don't even think about running again," Olympus said. "You've raised a lot of interest by returning here. The Magic Council has to ensure they neutralize any threats. As you pointed out, Witch Haven is in a fragile position, and its reputation has yet to be restored. You're partially responsible for that."

His colleagues sparked magic on their fingers, and I could see Thaddeus was desperate to blast me with a spell. I'd have to keep an eye on him.

"You three go back inside," I muttered to Hilda, Russell, and Nugget. "They won't let you come with me, and I don't want you getting in any trouble."

"We can't let them take you," Hilda said. "It's not fair."

"If I go in front of the full council, I'll have a chance to say my piece to other magic users. I could find a sympathetic ear among them. Lots of them knew Magda. She may still have allies." I lifted Hilda off my shoulder and placed her on the ground, then nodded at Nugget and Russell. "Keep an eye on things until I get back."

"If you come back." Nugget turned and stalked away.

Russell cawed several times before flying over to the trees. Hilda tapped her legs on the ground, before turning and scurrying away.

I was sad to see them go, but this was for the best. There was no way I was getting my familiars in any more hot water.

I turned back to Olympus. "Where do we need to go for this meeting?"

"Touch my arm. I'll transport us there," Olympus said.

I strode over and grabbed his arm. Thaddeus glared at me like I'd just committed a terrible crime by daring to touch his boss.

"Everyone link with me," Olympus said.

Thaddeus and his colleague touched Olympus, and he evoked a transportation spell.

The world tilted, and I grew dizzy as his magic folded around me. It smelt of the forest, with a faint hint of salt spray.

We arrived in a large, high-ceilinged chamber, with dark wood panels and a ring of seats around the outside. And all those seats were occupied by Magic Council members.

We were at the back of the room, so no one had seen us appear.

Thaddeus hurried away, while Olympus remained beside me.

"Hugo, inform the overseer of our arrival. Ask if we can be heard during any other business," Olympus said.

Hugo, the guy with the neat goatee, nodded and strode away.

"Catching me will be a feather in your cap," I said. "Will you get a big bonus for finally bringing the last Ash witch to heel?"

"No talking, or you'll disturb the meeting," Olympus said.

"You're in charge of this lot. Why does it matter if we disturb them?"

He sighed softly. "There's a lot you don't know about the Magic Council. I may head up a particular sector, but I'm by no means in charge of everything. Judge Zimmerman is proceeding over matters at this meeting, and he runs things in a specific way. He's also strict with rule breakers."

"What could he do to me? Take away my freedom? Threaten to remove my magic and turn me into a shadow? Destroy the home I was raised in?"

Olympus arched an eyebrow at me and shook his head.

I felt appropriately chastised by that stern glare, but it was a point worth making. I'd already hit rock bottom several times and somehow bounced off it. They couldn't do anything more to me.

I looked around the room. From where I stood, I could count over a hundred members of the Magic Council in attendance. It was a huge organization, covering all areas of magic and ensuring its safe use.

A murmuring began in the far right corner of the room. It drifted closer, and then heads turned in my direction.

"It looks like word is spreading fast about my arrival. I can't wait to meet my fans," I said.

There was a loud, dull thudding coming from somewhere in the room, and the murmuring stopped.

I leaned forward and saw Judge Zimmerman standing and peering around. He was a tall, wiry warlock, with a neat white beard and white hair that sat on his shoulders. His gaze stopped when it landed on me.

I resisted the urge to step back. The power resonating from him could be felt even from this distance.

"Indigo Ash. At last, we meet." Judge Zimmerman beckoned me closer.

I glanced at Olympus. I wasn't checking for his permission to move, but some reassurance would be no bad thing.

"You'd better go. It looks like he's changed the agenda just for you, and he normally hates change."

"Lucky me. I'd rather be in any other business, when people are packing up their papers and thinking about their next cup of coffee and the chocolate cookies on their desk."

"Get a move on," Olympus said. "And no smart talking the judge. Your fate is in his hands, so be nice."

"Will it make a difference if I am?"

"Indigo! Don't try his patience. You'll only regret it."

Judge Zimmerman pointed to a table and chairs set in front of the raised podium he stood at. I walked over, my legs stiff as if they were resisting my efforts. My mind was screaming at me to escape, but where could I go? I was surrounded by powerful magic users, and they all wanted to prevent me from causing trouble.

I stopped by the table and looked up at Judge Zimmerman.

He gave me a nod. "The rest of the agenda items are to be moved to our next meeting. We have something crucial to consider."

There were a few disgruntled mutters, but they quickly died away when the judge glared around the room.

"For those of you who don't know, the witch standing before us is Indigo Ash. When she was seventeen, along with her stepmother, Magda Ash, she murdered sixty-six people in Witch Haven."

There were several gasps, but most people simply grumbled. They most likely knew my history.

"Miss Ash, I'd hoped your time in rehabilitation and prison reformed you, but it seems that since your return to Witch Haven, the troubles there have intensified," Judge Zimmerman said.

I raised my hand and wiggled my fingers.

"This isn't a school, Miss Ash. You may speak when it is your time," Judge Zimmerman said. He lifted a finger. "And now is not that time. This is our opportunity to discuss your punishment."

"Strip her power," someone called out.

"She's dangerous. She shouldn't have any magic," another voice called.

"Send her back to rehab," a female voice said.

I turned, looking for the witch who'd just spoken, but I couldn't see her. At least there was one magic user in this room who thought I was worthy of a second chance.

There were lots more cries to strip me of my power and punish me. Judge Zimmerman let it go on for several minutes.

"That's enough." He smoothed a hand over his beard. "We all agree your previous sentencing was unsuccessful, and additional rehabilitation is unlikely to produce a different result."

"I'd take it if it was on offer. And rehab helped me the last time," I said.

"Watch your step. You haven't been told you can speak."

I jumped at the closeness of Olympus' voice. I hadn't realized he'd joined me by the table.

I looked at him. "But I need a chance to plead my case."

"Go ahead, Miss Ash," Judge Zimmerman said. "How will rehabilitation be different for you this time around?"

I met his steely pale blue gaze head on. "I'm different. I know I've bent a few rules since coming back to Witch Haven, but I've been helping a friend. Luna Grimstone is missing. She's been taken by a ghost. I'm trying to find her."

The judge shook his head. "That is not a matter for us to consider. Your illegal and potentially dangerous behavior is our focus."

Luna may not matter to him, but she was my priority. "What if I had proof the murders

I helped commit in the village were part of something darker?" I held up the journal. "Magda Ash was manipulated by a witch coven. She details everything in here. Read it. This will show you the source of your troubles, and it's not me."

There were more resentful murmurs from around the room.

Panic made my throat tighten as the flood of anger and resentment in the room became palpable. I was running out of options. They'd probably take this journal and destroy it without bothering to read it. The Magic Council weren't interested in knowing the truth, they just wanted to get rid of me.

I looked around the chamber, trying to find a friendly face, but all I saw were accusatory stares. Many of the members wouldn't even look at me.

I should have known it would end up like this, even though a tiny part of me still believed the Magic Council wanted the best for all magic users. That part of me was wrong.

Olympus stepped up beside me and cleared his throat. "Judge Zimmerman, if I may speak on behalf of Indigo."

I turned and stared up at him. Was he going to put the final nail in my coffin? If he told the judge I'd whacked him with a spell and run off, I really was a goner.

Olympus glanced at me, and I could read the warning in his eyes to keep quiet.

"Go ahead, Olympus," Judge Zimmerman said.

"Indigo is adamant there's a coven wanting to harm Witch Haven. May I suggest we look at the evidence she presents and hold off from passing her final sentence until then."

"Why would we do that?" Judge Zimmerman said. "We have her here. She has eluded us for too long. This is our opportunity to finish this unpleasant business."

"I don't disagree. But Indigo is fighting her own battle in Witch Haven. She was telling the truth about her missing friend, and I believe she wants to help her. She won't go anywhere until she's succeeded in that task. In the meantime, we can consider this new information, while we put Indigo to work. I believe she can help us with an ongoing problem."

Judge Zimmerman peered down at him. "Help us how?"

I was also interested in hearing the answer to that question.

"Indigo has connections with Ursa Wyrm." He shot me another glare.

There were more murmurs from the council members, and this time, they didn't sound so unhappy. Maybe some of them had met her.

"What's Ursa got to do with this?" I muttered to Olympus.

He ignored me and remained focused on the judge. "Indigo could deal with Ursa's... ongoing problem. And she's already been to Ursa's house to assess the current issue. Indigo could be a useful asset while we decide her fate. And we could even place her in the house to make it easier to monitor her."

I shook my head. "No way! I'm not going back to that nightmare house. And if I have anything more to do with Ursa, I'll kill her. She set her dolls on me, she lied about me, and she stole from me."

"Did you hear that? The Ash witch just admitted she wants to kill Ursa," someone called out. "She isn't safe."

I threw my hands up. "I was joking. I wouldn't kill Ursa." I probably was joking. Although I wouldn't mind whacking her with a painful spell. And I'd only kill her if she got really mean.

"This is your one opportunity to help Luna and maintain a degree of freedom," Olympus muttered under his breath. "Don't mess this up, or Judge Zimmerman will have you hauled out of here and you won't see daylight ever again."

"But it's Ursa Wyrm! You know what a nightmare she is."

"Silence, everyone," Judge Zimmerman said. "The problems with Gravesend Manor have been going on for many months. We've tried various solutions and nothing has placated Ursa. Perhaps we need to try another route. And if Miss Ash is already familiar with the... issues, she could be useful to us."

I stared at him, my mouth open. He was seriously thinking about locking me in the dark, spooky doll house of terror? That wasn't freedom. What was he hoping would be the outcome of this terrible decision? The dolls and gnomes would get rid of me for him, and I'd be removed from the next meeting agenda?

"If I'm useful to you, does that mean you'll be lenient with my sentencing?" I said.

"Don't push your luck," Olympus said.

Judge Zimmerman tapped a finger on the podium. "I'll be open-minded regarding your sentence if you tackle Ursa's problems. If you can take this trouble off our hands, it will be looked upon favorably."

I hesitated. I didn't have the time to waste on dealing with Ursa and her hexed dolls. I had to focus on finding Luna.

I looked at Olympus again. He raised his eyebrows at me. "It's either this or rehab, and then your power will be stripped. I know what I'd choose."

"But Luna's missing. I'm not going to stop searching for her just so I can tackle Ursa's spooky house of horrors."

"You won't have to. If you're discreet, you can do both. This is a lifeline you've been offered. You'd be an idiot not to take it."

My gaze ran over Olympus. Was he trying to help me, or simply setting me up for an epic fail?

"We're waiting for your answer, Miss Ash," Judge Zimmerman said. "You can remain in Witch Haven if you work on Ursa's problem. In the meantime, we will review the evidence you've presented to us, alongside your future sentencing."

"It's a more than fair deal, given your history," Olympus said.

I nodded. It was, and I had no option but to accept.

I looked the judge squarely in the eyes. "You're on. Sign me up for an extended stay in Ursa's creepy doll house."

Those dolls wouldn't know what hit them when I returned.

Chapter 10

I was still in shock as I was taken from the meeting room chamber. This hadn't been the plan. I wasn't here to help the Magic Council. They were supposed to hear me out so I could make progress on clearing my name and making things right for Magda.

But at least this option gave me a reprieve. And if I could solve Ursa's hex problem, or rather the problems she was causing the Magic Council, my outlook may not be so bleak.

Olympus walked alongside me in silence until we reached a large set of doors.

I turned to him. "Why did you help me back there?"

He glanced around, pushed open the doors, and gestured me to follow him. It was only when they closed and we were standing outside in an empty cobbled courtyard that he looked my way.

"I thought you wanted to remain a free witch."

"Of course. But ever since I returned to the village, you've been trying to arrest me. Why the change of heart?"

He lifted one shoulder. "Ursa's a pain in my butt. Her uncle sits on the Scrutiny Committee and oversees the standards maintained by Magic Council employees. Whenever Ursa has a problem, she runs straight to him, and he dumps it on someone else to deal with."

"And you're the latest victim of being dumped on?"

"You got it."

"So you've handed your problem on to me."

"Better that than a harsh sentence and an immediate loss of your power and freedom. Judge Zimmerman is most insistent that he's not bothered by the Scrutiny Committee, so we run around placating Ursa and her uncle."

"And you think I can solve her issues? I've already dealt with her dolls once. It didn't end so well. Not all of them survived."

"You must get this right, or you'll face the consequences."

I tipped back on my heels and peered into his emotionless face. "Is that the only reason you stood up for me in there?"

"What other reason could there be?" He held my gaze for a second too long, before gesturing to the main gate. "We'll go to Ursa's house immediately. We need to keep her updated, or she'll only cause more problems for Judge Zimmerman, and that means more problems for me."

"Or rather, me."

"You're getting good at this." His smirk turned into a full-on grin. Olympus was enjoying this.

"This is a mistake. Ursa will hate seeing my face again. She pretty much threw me out after I smoked her favorite killer doll."

"Then convince her you're an asset, not an issue. And I'll be there to ease any concerns she may have."

"You're coming with me?"

"I have no choice. Before we left, Judge Zimmerman assigned me as your guardian."

I wrinkled my nose. "You mean you'll be hanging around all the time watching my every move?"

"That's the plan. Aren't I the fortunate one?" He smiled slyly. "And while you're dealing with Ursa's issues, you're to remain in her house. That's part of the agreement."

"For good?"

"It'll be easier to track you if you have a single residence and aren't moving from place to place. And it's not forever, just until you fix her latest drama and give the judge some peace."

"You mean, I can't leave?"

"You may leave, providing you get my permission. But I need to know where you are at all times. The judge took a risk by giving you this assignment. Do not let him down. Or me."

I shook my head. I was still bemused as to why Olympus was taking this chance on me. "Ursa and her uncle must be horrors if you're gambling on me to sort this mess out."

"They are. Besides, we have nothing to lose. If you get this wrong, you'll simply be sentenced, as was the original plan."

"And if I get it right?"

We reached the gates. Olympus nodded to a guard on duty, and he opened them for us.

"If you get it right, then you can expect Judge Zimmerman to be fair. He'll be true to his word about taking your assistance into account when sentencing you."

"I may get to keep my powers?"

"Most likely. And if he's in a generous enough mood, he may even let you keep the house as well."

I gulped. "What house are you talking about?"

He snorted a soft laugh. "I know you're hiding Magda's house."

"No, I'm not." Technically, that was the truth. My awesome familiars had done all the hard work there. "You saw the rubble. The place went ka-boom days ago."

"I did. And it took me a while to figure out that the rubble was in the wrong place. I'm assuming you're hiding the house behind magical wards?"

Olympus sounded surprisingly calm for someone who'd figured out he'd been duped.

"What if I am?"

"Then it's another example of how powerful you are, and how careful we need to be around you." He surprised me by smiling. "Relax. I have no plans to knock down that house. Not at the moment, anyway. I can only imagine the strong magic hidden within those walls. If you'd wanted to do anything truly hideous to the village, you've had all the resources at your fingertips, and you'd have done it by now."

"Does that mean you think I'm not such a bad witch?"

"I'm on the fence about that. And you need somewhere to stay while you're in Witch Haven. It would be a shame to lose the magic and spells Magda collected over the years." We reached the end of the pathway.

His admission stunned me. I may get to keep my powers and my house. I really couldn't afford to get things wrong with Ursa. Not with so much riding on it.

I turned and looked back at the building we'd come out of. It was enveloped in such a thick mist, I could barely see it. "Where are we?"

"Don't concern yourself about that. The Magic Council moves around. It's risky to have meetings in the same place too often. There are many forces out there who'd like to get rid of the Council. I expect you're one of them."

"Nope. You can scrub me off the list of magic users planning to bring down the establishment. I don't hate the Magic Council. I hate what they did to me and Magda, but I put my hands up and admitted to what I'd done, and they imprisoned me based on the evidence. But..."

"But? You have something to say about the organization that just threw you a lifeline?"

"You threw me a lifeline." And I was still figuring out why. "I wish they'd loosen up. They seem so out of touch with the real world."

"Big organizations get like that. We become slow moving, and it takes too long for anything effective to happen."

"It sounds like you're making plans for a career change," I said. "Have you grown disillusioned with your employer?"

"There's no chance of that. My life is my work. And perhaps one day I really will rule this entire organization. Then things will be very different."

"That doesn't sound like much fun. There must be more to you than work."

Olympus smoothed a hand across his chin, but didn't speak. He reached out as if to take hold of my hand, but stopped and stepped away. "Your secret is safe with me. You can keep the house hidden. I don't want to see you homeless, and I wouldn't wish my worst enemy to have a permanent home with Ursa. But you must stay there while you deal with her issues."

I opened my mouth, then closed it again. Olympus kept on being nice to me. Did I trust him? After all, he was Magic Council, and a big part of my problem.

"Ah! There are your familiars." Olympus' gaze shifted away from me.

I turned around. "How did they know I was here? Wherever here is."

"I summoned them. I thought you may require backup when you move into Ursa's house."

I couldn't figure Olympus out. It was as if he'd had a personality transplant. And I had no idea what to say, so I said nothing.

Russell arrived first, giving a hearty caw and circling around my head several times.

"And just so you know, I will be looking into your claims of this dark witch coven," Olympus said.

"Perhaps I may borrow Magda's journal to read. I could find something you missed."

"Oh! That would be great, so long as you look after it. I couldn't find any names in this journal, but if I can get back to the house, I'll keep searching. Magda must have put more information about the coven somewhere." I handed over the journal.

He tucked it under his arm. "If there's any truth to your claim, I'll get to the bottom of it."

I blinked several times and nodded. I really couldn't get used to this new version of Olympus.

"You're free." Nugget trotted over and flicked his tail at me. "We thought we'd arrive to find you turned into a shadow, and have to drag your hollow, pointless body away and figure out what to do with it."

"Awww! You always say the sweetest things to me."

Hilda ran up my leg and onto my shoulder. "And you're talking to Olympus," she whispered in my ear.

I glanced at him. "We'll discuss that later. For now, I'm a sort of free witch, with a few conditions attached."

Russell flapped around my head, cawing happily, before settling on my other shoulder.

"How did you work out a deal with the Magic Council?" Nugget said. "I figured you were done for."

I glanced at Olympus, who'd moved a short distance away. "Well, I had some assistance. The Magic Council agreed to let me go, so long as I help them with the problems Ursa's having in her house."

"You'll help the witch who stole from you?" Nugget wrinkled his furry nose. "Why would we do that?"

"It was that option, or be locked up again," I said. "And once we're inside her house, we'll have the perfect chance to find out why she stole the ghost jar from us, and get it back."

Olympus cleared his throat and shot me a warning glare.

I lifted a hand. "I deserve to get back what's mine. Don't worry, I won't blast Ursa with magic unless she really annoys me. But I will do a little searching while her back is turned. I'm getting that ghost jar back. It could be important to finding Luna."

I looked at my familiars and smiled. This felt good. Now we were back together, we could make some progress.

"Be careful when you're at Ursa's house," Olympus said. "That place is full of unpleasant secrets."

I nodded. "I've already encountered a few. I'll be on my guard."

"Why is Olympus worried about your safety?" Hilda whispered.

That was an excellent question, and one I had no time to dwell on.

"When do we start?" Nugget said.

"Right away," Olympus said.

I shrugged. There was no time like the present. "How do you feel about making friends with more creepy possessed dolls?"

An hour later, and after a quick stop at Magda's house to grab a few essentials, I stood outside Gravesend Manor with Olympus and my familiars.

Olympus knocked on the door and stepped back. "Let me do the talking. Ursa needs to be handled sensitively."

"You can handle her as sensitively as you like, but she's no friend of mine," I said. "I'll deal with her hexing, or whatever it is, but I won't pretend we're friends."

"Just don't go killing anyone," Olympus said.

Ursa pulled open the door. She stared at me and frowned before her hard glare settled on Olympus. "What are you doing bringing her here?"

He gave a slight bow. "I have a proposition for you. Indigo specializes in assisting with problem hexes and hauntings."

I opened my mouth to protest but snapped it shut the second Olympus glared at me.

"And what's your point?" Ursa said.

"The Magic Council has hired Indigo on a freelance basis to assist you with your troubled dolls. I believe you expressed concerns to your uncle about them."

Ursa pursed her lips. "I did. But this won't do. She's already been here. She didn't help."

"That's not true. I located the problem and stamped on her," I said. "That was more than you did."

Ursa narrowed her eyes. "You left behind chaos and ruined Mary-Sue. I've only just finished fixing up that room and settling down my dolls."

"Indigo has assured the Magic Council she won't cause any trouble. And she'll be working under my strict guidance. I'm overseeing all matters in regard to this case. I'll also have guards outside your home, so if there are any problems, you can call on them for assistance." Olympus gestured at me. "And we also think it's best if Indigo stays here, so she's around to assess any trouble you have. She'll be on call night and day."

I wasn't happy about being under house arrest, or being at Ursa's beck and call, but I shouldn't be surprised this was happening. The Magic Council was a long way from ever trusting me, so why not use me for anything they could get? To them, I was just another problem to neutralize once I'd served my purpose.

Ursa was quiet as her cold stare tracked over me and my familiars. "I'm unhappy about sheltering a dark witch in my home. What if she tries to hurt me?"

"You know how to look after yourself. Don't pretend you have no power." I rested a hand on my hip.

Ursa continued to glare at me.

"Since Indigo returned to Witch Haven, she's been helping others in need. She assisted her friend during a troublesome haunting and has been cooperating with me and the Magic Council. I trust her to do the right thing when it comes to your problem," Olympus said.

Well, spank me with a broomstick and call me a moon nymph. Olympus was standing up for me yet again. Had he been given a potion that made him lighten up? I wasn't complaining if that was the case, but it would take a while to adjust to this new version.

Ursa crossed her arms over her chest. "I don't like this. But so far, the Magic Council has been most unhelpful. She can come inside, but this is only on a trial basis. And I will be watching to see how she does."

"She'll do fine," I said. "Just so long as you don't rile her too much. Then she can get angry and her magic gets out of control."

"No one needs to get angry," Olympus said sharply.

Ursa huffed out a breath. "Do you expect me to feed her and find her somewhere to sleep?"

I looked at the huge house which must have at least a dozen unused bedrooms. And Ursa lived alone, if you discounted the evil dolls and grumpy gnomes. "I'm sure you can squeeze me in somewhere. And I don't eat much."

There was a long pause. Ursa stared at me, and I stared back.

"Oh, very well. So long as you deal with my dolls. And by deal, I don't mean smash them to pieces."

I went to step inside and then looked back at Olympus. "Aren't you coming in?"

He shook his head, his gaze sliding to the side. "Ursa has a gnome problem I need to tackle."

"I've encountered the gnomes. They're not friendly. One of them threw a stone axe at me."

He leaned forward so his mouth was close to my ear. "I have a sledgehammer I intend to use on them. Go inside. And try not to kill each other."

"Stop dawdling," Ursa said from the hallway.

I hurried inside with my familiars, and the door slammed shut behind me. I jumped. It must have been the breeze, because Ursa was striding along the hallway in front of me, and there was no one else around.

"Follow me. I'll show you the house. I don't want you in most of the rooms, though. Stick to where I tell you."

"I need full access if I'm going to solve this problem. I'm not even sure what I'm dealing with yet. Is it a hex, a curse, a possession?" I jogged along behind her.

"To the left, you'll find the front floral parlor, games room, second entertainment room, dining room, and kitchen. To the right, there's the green front parlor, the library, the study, and the reading room."

"Wouldn't it make more sense to have the library and the reading room in the same place?" I said. "It must get annoying having to go find a book and then walk to another room to read it."

"No, it wouldn't. I don't want you going in either of those rooms."

"If I sense a malevolent presence in the rooms, am I allowed to go in?"

"Tell me if you sense anything, and I'll make that decision," Ursa said. "At the back of the house is the utility room, and several storerooms for supplies and dried goods. They're out of bounds, too. Let's go upstairs. I'll put you in the guest wing, in the room furthest from mine."

"That sounds perfect," Nugget whispered. "I'm already feeling bad having to breathe the same air as this harpy."

"I heard that," Ursa said. "And animals should be kept outside. I don't want my carpets shredded or soiled."

"These are my familiars. It's important they stay close. If I'm without them, I won't be able to do my job properly."

Ursa gave a most unladylike grunt. "If they put so much as a paw or a claw wrong, they're out. I don't care how important they are."

"I know where I'd like to put my paw," Nugget muttered.

"I heard that, too," Ursa said. "The wing to your left is my private wing. Don't go anywhere near the rooms on this side of the building. The right side is the guest wing."

"That's where the creepy dolls are located," Hilda said.

I nodded as I followed Ursa along a dimly lit corridor. The wallpaper had large faded pink roses on it, and the carpet underneath was a washed out deep blue. This must once have been a luxurious house, but now carried an atmosphere of neglect and despair.

Ursa headed back to the top of the stairs. "That's enough of a tour. I suppose you want dinner?"

I hadn't eaten in what felt like days. "If it's no trouble."

"Of course, it's trouble. I'll make you a sandwich. You can eat in the kitchen. I always turn in early, so you'll have to entertain yourself."

"Can we use the entertainment room?" Nugget said. "What games do you have?"

"No. Stay out of there."

Nugget grumbled under his breath all the way down the stairs.

Ursa led us into the kitchen. It was a dark room, with small, high up windows set in one wall. The units were black, and the gray granite work surface glittered.

Ursa dumped bread and cheese on the counter, along with a knife and a plate. "Don't leave any mess. I'll come back for you and show you to your room once I've made it up." She turned and stomped out.

"This is going to be so much fun," Nugget said.

"It'll be okay." I sliced off some bread and made a sandwich. "We'll figure out the hex or curse, neutralize it, and get out as quickly as we can. We'll be here a couple of days at the most."

Nugget froze and his eyes widened.

I turned and grimaced as I spotted a dozen stuffed animals adorning one wall. I turned my back on them and ate standing up, while tossing pieces of bread and cheese to everyone.

"That fox with the bug eyes is moving," Nugget whispered. "And it just snarled at me."

"It's stuffed. It's just a trick of the light." I chewed faster. I wasn't paying any attention to the freaky stuffed critters behind me. If I didn't acknowledge them, they couldn't hurt me.

"It isn't," Hilda said. "Several are moving. They're creeping our way. And I don't think they want to make friends."

I stuffed the rest of the sandwich into my mouth and turned to face the animals. I couldn't see anything different about them.

"I haven't taken my eyes off that fox," Nugget said. "Foxes eat cats when they're desperate."

"That one can't eat a thing. It doesn't have a stomach," I said.

"But it's living in a hexed house," Hilda said. "We should leave before they make us their dinner."

A movement on the top shelf caught my eye. I looked up to see a particularly malevolent hedgehog glowering at me. It bared its tiny teeth and growled.

"You're right. Let's get out of here." I yanked open the kitchen door to find Ursa standing outside. "Have you been there this whole time?"

"Of course not! I've been busy sorting your room."

"Great! We're ready for bed." I glanced at the stuffed animals. "Why don't you show us the room?"

Ursa peered over my shoulder. "This way. I put out towels and fresh bedding. You can make the bed up yourself."

"No problem." I hurried away from the kitchen.

"Do we get beds?" Nugget asked.

"You can sleep in the shed in the yard," Ursa said.

"The floor is fine," I said. "They don't like sleeping outside."

Ursa grumbled to herself. "They're not allowed on the bed."

"Of course." I winked at Nugget. They were absolutely sleeping on my bed if they wanted to.

"This way." Ursa led us up the stairs and along a corridor.

"Before we fix a work plan for hex elimination, I wonder if you could do me a favor," I said.

"It's most unlikely. What is it?"

I hurried along beside her. "You know about Luna going missing?"

"I do. She's still not shown up?"

"No, and I need to focus on her disappearance. The longer she's missing, the less chance I have of finding her."

"And? Spit it out. What's the favor?"

"I'm getting close to a breakthrough, but I won't be able to make any progress unless she's my priority. I promise, I'll help with your hexing as soon as I can, but I've got to keep the pressure on so Luna is found. I've already made contact with her, so I know she's alive. I just don't know where she is."

Ursa turned and shook her head. "I do have sympathy for Luna's situation, but you're my assistant now. The Magic Council assigned you to me."

"And I will help you, but Luna's in trouble. She's scared and alone. She needs me."

"I need you. No, it's out of the question. Unless you want to go back to prison, you'll do what you've been tasked to." Ursa stopped so abruptly, I almost walked into her. "It still boggles the mind that the Magic Council is utilizing your services, but I suppose they know best. Still, I'll be bringing this to my uncle's attention. He needs to know about this bizarre move. Using criminals to help upstanding members of the community. Whatever next?"

I glowered at her back as she led me to the end of the corridor.

"This is your room." She pushed open the door, a smirk on her face.

I stared into the room, my stomach dropping. Ursa had wedged a tiny single bed in the middle of the hexed dolls' room.

Her smirk widened. "I doubt you'll get much sleep, so you can start your investigation immediately."

Chapter 11

My eyes were watering because I hadn't blinked for so long. Every time I tried to get any sleep in my terrifying new bedroom, a doll moved. It may be just an arm or a leg, or beady eyes would swivel in my direction, but these dolls were up to something, and the outcome would be bad for all of us.

"I think this is a positive sign," Hilda whispered from her position on my head.

"What is?" I had to lower the covers so my voice wasn't muffled.

"The dolls haven't gone for an all-out attack. They're anxious around you. They must remember what we did the last time we were here."

"They may be anxious, but there's a heck of a lot more of them than there are us."

"I'm not staying here a second longer," Nugget said. "I've already had my tail bitten twice."

"Are you sure that isn't fleas?" I said.

His whiskers bristled, and he hissed at me. "I don't have fleas."

"Fleas don't like the taste of him," Hilda said. "He tastes too much like the grave."

"I taste sublime. But I'm done with being stared at by these freaky dolls," Nugget said. "Can't we explore the rest of the house for the ghost jar? Or just get out of here while we're still breathing."

I checked the time. It was two in the morning. We'd only been here a few hours, but I wouldn't get a wink of sleep if I stayed here all night, waiting for the dolls to regroup and get us.

"I'm done, too. Let's get out of here and find Storm and Odessa. We can work on finding Luna and be back here before dawn. Ursa won't even know we snuck out."

I headed to the window and peered into the dark night. A full moon looked back at me. It bathed the yard in a stark, shadowy glow. I grabbed my jacket and boots and put them on. I'd gone to bed fully clothed, feeling too vulnerable to wear the red stripy pajamas I'd brought with me. You couldn't kick dolly backsides so easily in comfy nightwear.

"There's a sloped roof beneath this window," Hilda said. "We should be able to get out without having to go through the house and waking Ursa."

"Or the stuffed animals lurking in the kitchen," Nugget said.

I opened the window. "Russell, you go out first and scout ahead. Make sure the guards aren't watching." I hadn't seen the Magic Council guards appear, but knowing Olympus, they'd be out there somewhere.

Russell gave a soft caw and swept out through the open window. A moment later, he was back. He bobbed his head up and down and then flew off.

"It looks good," Hilda said. "I'll go next."

I held her over the window ledge, and she used a string of webbing to get down to the roof, before disappearing out of sight.

Nugget went next. He hopped out and gracefully landed on the roof, before sliding down and over the edge.

My exit was less elegant. The window was small, so it was a squeeze to get through. I caught my foot on the windowsill and almost pitched out headfirst.

I did a flailing somersault and skidded down the roof, grabbing the guttering at the last second and clinging to it. I expected it to break, and I'd plunge to the ground, alerting the guards and Ursa to what we were up to.

I took a few breaths, trying to calm my racing heart. I'd just started swinging my legs back and forth to get on the roof, when my hand slipped off. I squeaked. I couldn't hold on one-handed.

Russell swooped over my head. He caught hold of the back of my jacket in his talons and frantically flapped his large wings.

"What are you doing? You can't carry me. I'm way too heavy for you." I let out another squeak as my other hand slipped.

Instead of falling, I was... flying. Well, almost. I couldn't believe it. Russell was carrying me. Okay, it was more like a slow descent to the ground, but he was in control.

I landed with a grunt, but I was upright, and no bones got broken.

I turned, wrapped Russell in my arms, and kissed him on the head. "You're the best bird familiar a witch could ever have."

He squawked and nuzzled against me, before wriggling loose and flying away.

"When you've finished messing around, you need to follow me," Nugget whispered. "There's something weird going on in the grounds."

"It's probably the gnomes," I said. "Did you see Russell save my life?"

"That bird is ridiculous. He still thinks he's an eagle."

"He is. He's a magnificent, gladiatorial eagle. He just comes in a small black feathery package."

Russell soared over my head and dipped his wing in response to my praise.

"You'll give him a big ego if you keep talking like that," Nugget said. "This way. I heard chanting, and that's rarely a good sign."

I checked around to make sure the Magic Council guards were nowhere near, then followed Nugget, Hilda, and Russell into the gloom of some nearby trees.

As we continued creeping through them, I slowed and tilted my head. It sounded like lots of low, deep male voices saying the same thing over and over again in a language I didn't understand.

"We should leave them to it," I whispered. "Maybe the gnomes are having a celebration we don't know about. They won't be happy if we blunder our way in and spoil their fun."

"It's not just chanting I can hear. There's another voice mixed in with it," Nugget said. "An angry voice."

The chanting grew louder as we drew nearer. I stopped behind a large tree and poked my head around the side. My eyebrows shot up. There were twenty gnomes in a circle, their little arms held out. In the middle of the circle, Olympus was tied to the ground. And he was naked. There were symbols painted on his chest in black, but I'd gotten more than an eyeful when I first saw him, so didn't make any more attempts to see what they were.

"What are the gnomes doing to Olympus?" Hilda was up on my shoulder, taking in the scene. She didn't seem fazed by the lack of clothing.

I shielded my eyes so I couldn't see Olympus in all his glory and looked again. "It's nothing good. Not if he's tied down."

"Several of the gnomes have knives," Nugget said.

"They could be preparing to make a sacrifice," I said.

No one spoke as the chanting died. The largest of the gnomes stepped forward. He had on a green hat with a feather sticking out the top. Other than that, he was also naked.

"We're gathered here tonight, brothers, to present an offering. Our home has been in distress for many years, and we've been unable to placate the darkness. It will only spread if we don't act now. We cannot allow our home to be destroyed."

The rest of the gnomes nodded and swayed from side to side.

He raised his arms over his head. "I speak directly to the darkness that has come to Witch Haven. We offer you this warlock to appease your anger. We hope you consider this a worthy sacrifice, and will leave us in peace."

"They're going to kill Olympus," Hilda whispered. "It sounds like the gnomes have been having problems of their own."

I chewed on my bottom lip. I was tempted to let them carry on with their planned sacrifice. Olympus was a thorn in my side. But he'd just stood up for me in front of the Magic Council. He'd done the deal that meant I walked out of there with my powers intact and could continue searching for Luna. I owed him.

Hilda beat her legs on my shoulder. "Are you going to let the gnomes kill Olympus?"

"Um, I'm thinking about it. That head gnome could have a point. Maybe this darkness needs a blood sacrifice to appease it. It's not an uncommon ritual in some magic practices."

"You need to make up your mind if you're going to help him," Nugget said. "The gnomes are about to start stabbing."

Two gnomes approached Olympus with their knives held out.

Russell settled on my shoulder and nudged me with his beak.

"I'm still thinking. This could be our chance to get away. The Magic Council will still punish me, but with Olympus out of the picture, they'll need time to regroup. He's a key figure in the organization. Lose him and there'll be chaos."

"Get away to where?" Hilda said. "You've already decided this is your home, unless you've changed your mind. Don't say you're thinking about leaving us again?"

Russell jabbed me hard with his beak.

"Ouch! No, I mean, not really. I just thought for a second that it could be an option. You could all come with me."

"You can't let Olympus die," Hilda said. "He's in trouble. Look at him."

"I'm trying really hard not to. He's not got anything on."

"I see no problem with that. He's an attractive man. Did you see his abs? You could do a lot worse," Hilda said.

"Hilda! I'm not interested in Olympus Duke. He's annoying, and he keeps trying to arrest me."

"He's annoying and attractive," Hilda said. "You must help him."

"The time is right. The sacrifice is to be made," the head gnome said. "Brothers, you may begin the ritual of a thousand cuts."

I winced. That would be a horrible way to die. I sucked in a breath and stepped forward. "Wait! What claim do you have over this warlock?"

The gnomes turned toward me.

Hilda tapped my shoulder in approval. Russell cawed and flew off to settle in a tree, while Nugget stayed back, regarding the gnomes with narrowed eyes.

"Who are you to interrupt this sacred event?" the head gnome said, gesturing for silence among the grumbling gnomes.

"My name is Indigo Ash, the last witch in the Ash witch coven. I have a claim over this warlock. You have no right to take him from me."

There was more muttering among the gnomes, and several of them looked fearful, suggesting they knew my reputation.

The head gnome walked over. "I'm Bumble Redstock. We know of your connection to the village. What is your claim, Ash witch?"

"We... we have an association."

"An association? Elaborate."

I caught Olympus' gaze. His face was pale and sweating, and now I was closer, I spotted several wounds on his torso. He really was in trouble.

"We're partners. We're helping each other in a mutually beneficial arrangement."

"This warlock is your partner? I wasn't aware he had a connection with a powerful witch," Bumble said.

"It's a new thing. We're taking it slowly and testing the waters. We're not even sure we like each other yet," I said.

"If you don't like him, offer him to us. We need this ritual to work. We've tried so many things to appease the darkness. Nothing is effective, and we grow desperate for peace," Bumble said.

"I wish I could hand him over to you, but I can't. We have a deal in place. That's not something I can break."

"But we must have an offering for the darkness." Bumble's gaze grew anxious. "How about one of your familiars? Surely you don't need all three of them."

Nugget hissed behind me.

"No, they can't be used. Does it have to be a blood sacrifice? Are you sure that'll work?"

"No! But everything else has had no impact. And blood is powerful."

"Have you tried food offerings? Or perhaps something delicious to drink?" I had no idea if it would make any difference, but many magical beings could be swayed with their favorite treats.

"Not yet." Bumble turned to the other gnomes. "Why has no one suggested a food offering?"

They all looked at each other and shrugged.

"I'll do you a deal," I said. "If you release Olympus, I'll supply you with the best fermented honey mead in the village." Gnomes loved potent, sweet alcohol. And if an offering of mead had no effect, they could all get drunk and forget their worries for a short while.

There were excited murmurs among the naked gnomes.

"How much mead?" Bumble said. "This darkness won't be happy with a small sample."

"Twenty barrels."

"A hundred. Enough for everyone."

"That's a lot of mead," I said. "How about thirty?"

The gnomes gathered together and talked over each other as they debated my offer.

Bumble pulled back and headed toward me. "Seventy-five barrels in exchange for this warlock's life."

It was still a lot of booze, but it would keep them quiet and out of trouble. "Agreed. And thank you. I appreciate you giving me your sacrifice. Although I'm interested to know what's troubling you that you thought a warlock's blood would solve your worries."

Bumble glanced over his shoulder at his companions. "Release the warlock. Return him to this witch." He looked back at me. "These are worrying times. We must quiet the darkness."

"Do you know where this darkness is coming from?"

His flinty-eyed gaze ran over me. "Ever since you and Magda attacked the village, things have been unsettled. At first, it was only small matters, things that could be dismissed. But gnomes are watchers, and we miss nothing. We recorded matters and were careful to ensure the problems didn't impact on our community. But over the last eighteen months, it's been impossible to avoid."

"I'm sorry you're going through this. I never intended for there to be long lasting problems because of what happened that day."

Bumble lifted his pointed chin. "You were a young witch. And you seem different. Are you... recovered?"

"I'm a work in progress. But I'm working on fixing things for everyone in Witch Haven."

"That's good to hear. We don't want to lose our home. But if things continue the way they are, we'll have no choice but to abandon Witch Haven."

"And Ursa?" I said.

He snorted, and the other gnomes laughed. "Ursa lives here because we let her. Ignore what she tells you about us. We're in charge of these grounds, and we allow her to walk around unharmed. She doesn't control us, although we permit her to think she does. If she ever stepped out of line, I'd remind her who was in charge."

I grinned. "It sounds like you know Ursa well."

"Unfortunately, I do." Bumble peered up at me. "Are you working with this warlock to ensure the village remains protected?"

Olympus stumbled over, clutching the wounds on his chest. He held a large clump of moss over his groin.

My cheeks grew warm, and I looked away. "Yes! Definitely. Among other things."

"Then I wish you every success." Bumble gestured at Olympus. "And here is your reward. I hope you use him well."

"I, um, I have no plans to use Olympus for anything," I said.

"You should. He'd make a fine stud. And since you're the last of the Ash witches, you must have plans to continue the family line. Make use of this strapping warlock, and you'll have incredibly powerful children."

Olympus grunted as he staggered past me. "Let's get out of here, before they turn me into a pin cushion."

I raised a hand to the gnomes. "As soon as I've sorted your mead delivery, I'll get it sent over."

"We'll be waiting," Bumble said. "And if you don't deliver, we know where you live."

I had no doubt the gnomes would descend on my house in their full fury if I didn't bring them their booze.

I turned and hurried after Olympus, gesturing for my familiars to follow. I kept my gaze on the back of his head, not wanting to leer at his bare backside, even though it was a fine view.

"He must work out," Hilda whispered.

"Shush! Or he'll think you have a crush on him."

She jiggled on my shoulder. "I'm not the one with the crush."

Olympus ducked behind a tree and pulled out his clothes. "Give me a minute."

"You're injured. Do you need treatment?" I said.

"Good idea. Then you can get a closer look at his muscles," Hilda said.

I glared at her. "I'll offer you to the gnomes if you don't quieten down."

She simply waggled her legs at me.

"I'll be fine. I've got healing potions on me." Olympus emerged from behind the tree a moment later, adjusting his jacket. He reached into his pocket, pulled out a bottle of purple liquid, and downed it. He shuddered as he was engulfed in a pale purple mist. It swirled around his torso for several minutes.

"Feeling better?" I asked.

"I'll live." He glanced over my shoulder at the gnomes. "If you hadn't shown up, I'd be dead by now. You could have left me. Why did you help?"

"Because... I'm not actually sure. I guess it's because you helped me when I went before the Magic Council. You spoke up for me."

"Because it was the right thing to do." Olympus shrugged. "Although I'm puzzled as to what you're doing out here. Aren't you supposed to be in the house investigating Ursa's hex?"

"Oh! I was. But it was quiet, so—"

"You decided to sneak off. You were planning to come back, I hope?"

"Of course. I will help Ursa."

"Then let's go back to the house. We can deal with Ursa's issue together. I'm done with these gnomes. And I'm not convinced they won't try to blood let me again."

"No! I need to find Luna. The house is quiet. Ursa's hex will wait until the morning."

He shook his head. "We had a deal. We're going back in the house. But you won't be alone, since I'm coming with you. We can work on this together. After all, aren't I your new stud partner?"

Chapter 12

I blushed and turned away, but not before missing the gleam of amusement in Olympus' eyes. Was he flirting with me?

"Bumble didn't mean that. He got confused when I said we were partners. He thought…" I waved my hand in his general direction.

"I know exactly what Bumble thought. And why not? You're an attractive witch with power. That will get you noticed by many warlocks."

"Sure it does. I'm chasing the suitors away with a flaming broomstick."

He laughed. "Are you saying you're not interested in me as a potential stud?"

I turned back to him. "Stop calling yourself that. It's weird."

"No weirder than being stripped naked by a bunch of marauding gnomes and having beetle dung symbols painted on my chest." His smile made him too handsome for his own good.

"Yeah, that is odd. So… shall we go inside?"

"In a minute." His smile turned sly. "I haven't heard of you bringing anyone special back to the village."

Was he for real? Olympus was asking about my dating life? Had he forgotten I'd been locked up most of the time I'd been away from Witch Haven? And then I'd hidden in a hovel of an apartment, not wanting anything to do with the rest of the world.

"Does your silence mean there is someone special? Or is it complicated?" Olympus said.

"My silence means it's none of your business. Let's not focus on my love life." I had to get control of this situation. "I'm more interested in finding out why you want us to work together? You don't have to help me with Ursa's problem."

The gleam in his eyes faded. "I do. This is business, and the Magic Council expect results."

"And that's all?" Olympus' flirting had me flustered, and that was something I wasn't used to. But I couldn't lose sight of who he really was. He may be good-looking, but he wanted to take me down. A few kind words and a nice smile, wasn't changing how I felt about him.

"You already know Ursa is a problem for the Magic Council. We need her dealt with. We have other business to deal with other than her myriad problems that plague us on a daily basis."

"Like the darkness Bumble mentioned?" I said. "It seems every magic user in Witch Haven is struggling. Is that true?"

Olympus brushed dirt off one sleeve. "He spoke the truth."

"And what has the Magic Council been doing to deal with it?"

"Tracking you. We thought you were the source."

"But you're having doubts?"

He nodded slowly. "I was as convinced as everyone else that when you were taken out of the equation, things would settle. I believed you were the linchpin."

"So kill me and you remove the power source," I said. "Why don't you do just that? Test your theory."

"Because... I'm not so sure, anymore. You were different to how I expected. You're not the young, headstrong witch who was arrested all those years ago. I'd just joined the Magic Council when you were caught, but I read all the files on you, and everything I heard had me convinced."

"And now we've met, you think I'm a white witch personified?"

He snorted a laugh. "Hardly. But I'm less certain. And I don't like feeling uncertain. If you're not the cause of this darkness, then there's something else out there that we've yet to discover."

"I've discovered it. You should believe Magda's journal entry," I said. "There's no reason she'd lie to me. You need to look for this dark witch coven. Find the witch behind the magic that ruined Magda and me."

He nodded again. "If they are the problem, then we need to move quickly, before the darkness becomes too great to control."

"We? You're suggesting we work together?"

"I'm not your enemy, Indigo. But I am on the side of justice. I follow the clues, and at the time, they led me straight to you. However, now I've gotten to know you and learned of the coven's possible interference, I don't mind admitting I could be wrong."

Once again, he'd stunned me into silence. Not many people could do that.

"Perhaps we could work together to solve this mystery." A slow smile spread across his face when I still didn't speak. "Would that be so terrible?"

My familiars had remained silent until this point. Hilda did a tap dance on my shoulder, while Russell cawed and flapped his wings as he swooped down from a tree. Nugget made no comment.

"I guess it could work," I stammered. "Although I don't completely trust you. What if this is a trick?"

"It's not. Let's say we trust each other fifty percent for now. That's a good base to begin with," he said. "And since we half trust each other, there's something you need to know."

"Another problem in Witch Haven?"

"It's another problem for Witch Haven." Olympus' lips thinned. "The Magic Council is considering removing the village from existence."

I squinted, not sure I'd heard him right. "How do you remove an entire village?"

"This area has become tainted with darkness, and it's spreading at an increasingly rapid rate. We have to contain the menace. It can't be allowed outside the boundaries of the village. If it gets out, it'll contaminate other magic communities."

"What are they planning to do, drop a magic bomb on the place and pretend it never existed?"

"Something like that. It'll be a combination of erasing memories, relocating villagers, and then razing the place to the ground. The Council is taking an initial vote on this matter soon. If the majority are in favor of erasing the village from the history books, it could all happen by the end of the year."

"That's not fair. The whole village shouldn't disappear because of one hexed apple."

"We're talking about lots of very hexed, toxic apples. This darkness could contaminate anything it comes into contact with. The issue hasn't been decided yet, but it's one option. One of very few."

"Do you approve of this option?"

Olympus shook his head. "I'm certain we can save this place, but we're up against the clock to do so."

"Then we're in agreement for once. We must save Witch Haven."

"And we can do it better together," he said. "If you're willing, I'll work with you. And I'll make sure the Magic Council stay off your back, so we can continue to hunt this darkness."

"Does that include making sure I get time to find Luna?" There'd be no deal if he wanted me to focus on his interests first.

"Of course. She's been caught up in this. It wasn't her fault. We'll have time to find your friend. But first, we tackle Ursa's problem. Let's go inside and see how things stand."

I hesitated, but only for a second, before nodding. An ally on the inside of the Magic Council couldn't be rejected. Having Olympus on my side would make things much easier. He had access to huge amounts of resources, powerful magic, and contacts.

"Lead the way, stud," I said.

He chuckled as he headed to the front door of Gravesend Manor and entered.

I followed close behind with my familiars. There were no lights on in the house, and it was still before dawn, so the place was gloomy and unwelcoming.

We both cast light balls over our heads and spent a couple of minutes looking around.

A high-pitched giggle emerged from the shadows. It was followed by small running feet tapping across the wooden floorboards.

"The creepy dolls sound like they're on the loose and feeling feisty," I muttered. "Watch out for them. They may be small, but they're deadly. Almost as bad as those gnomes."

"Don't remind me about them," Olympus grumbled. "I'll be having words with Bumble. He knows who I am, but he intended to sacrifice me, anyway."

"They must have been desperate to grab you."

He let out a sigh. "They were. That's why I didn't have anyone arrested."

I arched an eyebrow. "Is that the real reason? Or is it because you realized twenty angry gnomes with knives were too much to take on alone?"

Olympus gave a soft snort. "That was also at the back of my mind."

Something hard and smooth brushed the back of my leg. I yelped as a sharp pain flared up my calf. I hopped around on one leg and turned, glimpsing a white petticoat fading into the shadows.

"Are you okay?" Olympus grabbed my elbow as I continue to hop.

I lifted one hand and inspected it. Blood had seeped through my jeans. "They're trying to hobble us. Crouch down. We need to know where these little terrors are coming from. And watch out for the one named Mary-Sue. I'm not sure if she survived, but she's leading this gang."

"What does she look like?"

"About two foot high, with red curls, a white dress, and an evil look in her eyes, like she's thinking about chewing off your arm the second your back is turned. She may be a bit charred around the edges."

"Got it."

Russell flew around, hunting out dolls, while Hilda remained on my shoulder.

Nugget mooched off into the shadows, looking like he didn't have a care in the world.

"Nugget, be careful, or you'll find yourself saddled up and the dolls riding you like a show pony," I whispered.

He flicked his tail in response and disappeared.

There was the sound of more small running feet, and something clattered to the floor above my head.

"I think I've seen Mary-Sue," Olympus whispered. "She's up ahead. She went in a room on the right-hand side."

"Let's get after her. If we can grab her, we can question her to find out what she wants." I crept along on my tiptoes behind Olympus.

He reached the reading room and inched the door open. He ducked back and nodded. "She's in here."

"We'll go in and shut the door, so she's trapped and backup can't get to her."

Olympus nodded. We ducked into the room, and I shut the door softly behind me. He reached for the light switch on the wall and then nodded at me.

I gave him a thumbs up. I crouched, ready to lunge at Mary-Sue the second I saw her.

The overhead light flicked on. Mary-Sue stood in the middle of the room, a snarl of rage on her face. Her tiny hands were in fists as she lunged toward me.

I met her head on, grabbing a handful of her silky red hair and yanking it hard. "Not so fast, Bride of Chucky. You need to tell us why you're here."

The doll squeaked and writhed, trying to get away from me, but I had her in a tight grip. She flailed her legs and pounded my hand with her cold fists.

"I'm not letting you go until you talk. I know you can. Why are you harassing Ursa?"

Mary-Sue stopped struggling. She turned her creepy face my way and blinked her eyes. A single tear ran down one cheek. "I'm trapped."

"What are you? Did a hex bring you to life?" I was unmoved by the fake waterworks.

Olympus walked over and joined me. "Magic users sometimes utilize dolls to confine other supernatural creatures." He ran his hands over Mary-Sue.

She giggled. "That tickles."

Olympus frowned. "I don't get a sense of what she is."

"Has a supernatural been hexed and placed into the body of this doll, or has someone hexed this doll so she comes alive and causes chaos?"

"It's impossible to tell." He stared at the doll. "Tell us your name. We may be able to release you once we know who you are."

"I'm only young. I died when I was a child."

"Stop lying," I said. "You're not a child. Or if you are, you're the daughter of a demon. You're making Ursa's life miserable, and mine."

"I'm lonely. I want to play. Ursa never lets us play."

"You're not playing. You're messing with people's lives. It ends now. Reveal yourself, and we'll set you free so you can leave this place. You're going, whether it's by your choice or we have to force you out."

"Maybe she can't leave if someone forced her into this doll," Olympus said. "Are you trapped? Tell us who you are."

The doll went limp for a second, before her head turned to Olympus. "My name is Bloom."

He took a step back, and the color drained from his face.

"Does that name mean something to you?" I said.

Olympus shook his head, but his hand was trembling as it went to his mouth. "Why did you use that name?"

"It's my name. It's the name my parents gave me. I was such a good girl. And I loved my daddy. I miss him."

Olympus sucked in a breath, and it came out shaky.

"Do you know who this is?" I said to him.

He was staring at the doll, his eyes full of tears, but he didn't answer.

I shook my head and focused back on Bloom. So much for working as a team. "It does feel like a hex has been put on this doll. This isn't a haunting. Someone with a grudge against Ursa could have arranged this. They knew she collected old dolls and planted this one for her to find. Ursa said it was the first time she'd bought a doll from this particular seller, so maybe the whole thing was a setup. I imagine she rubs a lot of people the wrong way, so our list of suspects could be long."

Olympus grunted and cleared his throat. "You... you could be right. Although..."

"What's wrong with you?" He was still pale and shaky.

"Why aren't you saving me? Why aren't you looking for me anymore?" Bloom said.

Olympus stammered a few unintelligible words, before reaching for the doll. "I am. And I'm sorry. I've never stopped looking."

He was freaking me out almost as much as Mary-Sue. "What's going on? Who is Bloom to you?"

"Give her to me," Olympus said. "I'll take her somewhere safe."

"Mary-Sue doesn't need to be somewhere safe. She needs to be interrogated."

"She's a child. An innocent." Olympus went to stroke the doll's cheek, but I moved her out of the way.

"No, you're not taking her anywhere. And you're being weird. You should get out of here. Maybe this doll is influencing you. The hex could affect the people around her, although I feel fine. You, however, are acting crazy. Back away from the evil doll, Olympus. I'll deal with her."

"No! You don't know what you've got. Give her to me, now." Olympus made a grab for the doll, but I dodged out of his way.

"Get a grip of yourself. She's messing with you. You've fallen under Mary-Sue's power. This thing is evil. Leave the room. I'll get rid of her."

"You're not touching Bloom. She belongs to me. She's mine." He grabbed for her again.

Russell squawked and dive-bombed Olympus, who ducked to avoid being scratched.

I backed away until the couch was between me and Olympus. "We should destroy her. She's not doing you any good."

"You won't hurt her. I must keep her safe. I failed her before." He held out his hands, pain and bewilderment clear on his face.

"I'm sorry, Olympus, but it's for the best." I smashed Mary-Sue into the fireplace, and she shattered into a dozen pieces.

Olympus raced over and grabbed the sharp pieces of porcelain and torn dress. "Why? Why did you do that?"

"Because Mary-Sue was making you act like an idiot. That thing wasn't going to tell us anything. She was being controlled by magic, and it was getting to you."

"She's... dead," Olympus roared. He reared up and grabbed me around the throat. "Why do you always have to cause trouble? Wherever you go, you're always destroying things. You destroyed Bloom."

Hilda leaped off my shoulder and sank her fangs into Olympus' hand. Russell continued to dive-bomb him, squawking and scratching his face, but neither attack had any effect.

"Stop! You're hurting me." I formed a fireball in my hand and held it over my head. "Don't make me use this on you."

His gaze met mine. He dropped his hands, and his shoulders sank as he backed away.

I gasped in a breath and closed my hand, extinguishing the fireball. "Olympus, what's the matter? The second the doll said the name Bloom, you fell apart."

He turned away, his back to me as he stared at the fireplace. Several seconds ticked by. "My daughter's name is Bloom."

"Oh! I didn't know you had any children."

"Just the one. She's eight years old. She... she disappeared three years ago."

My breath whooshed out of me. "I'm so sorry. I had no idea. What happened to her?"

"Bloom was stolen. I'm no longer with her mother, and it was my turn to look after her. As usual, my work interfered. I was dealing with a complicated case and working on new evidence. I had to visit a crime scene, so I took Bloom with me."

"What kind of crime are we talking about?" I had no kids, but even I baulked at the idea of taking a little one to somewhere dangerous.

"It was nothing bad. A robbery at a country house. I thought she'd enjoy taking a ride and seeing a new place. The owner had horses, which she loves." He hunched forward. "I turned my back for no more than twenty seconds, and she was gone."

I had the urge to hug him, but remained where I was. "That's a terrible thing to happen. But you can't think that doll contained the spirit of your daughter? Is Bloom... is she dead?"

Olympus turned back, and the haunted look on his face made my heart ache. "I don't know if she's dead or alive. That could have been her. It sounded like her. It sounded like my Bloom. I had a chance to speak to her, but that's gone because you destroyed the doll. That was the vessel she was using to communicate with me."

"No, that wasn't your daughter. That was the hex messing with you. It exploited your weakness. Some magic preys on weakness. You know this. Don't let it trick you."

"You don't know that wasn't Bloom. You didn't give me a chance to speak to her. You took that opportunity away from me." He pointed at the fragments of doll.

I walked over and rested a hand on his shoulder. "I know this will be hard to hear, but your daughter was never in Mary-Sue. It was just a creepy doll."

Olympus shrugged off my hand and stepped away. "You know nothing about me or my life. It was a mistake trying to work with you. You bring nothing but chaos and trouble." He headed to the door, yanked it open, and walked out.

I stared after him, helplessness running through my veins like a ruined spell on all Hallows Eve.

What the heck was I supposed to do now?

Chapter 13

I jerked awake and wiped the back of my hand against my mouth.

"Don't move." Nugget's butt was an inch from my face, his tail raised and bushy.

I took a very shallow breath and moved my gaze from side to side. We were back in the creepy dolls room. It was the only room in this house I'd been able to find a bed, and I'd been exhausted after my confrontation with Mary-Sue, and then having to deal with Olympus going off the rails.

I didn't think I'd sleep once I settled in, but I must have dozed off. Now, with a cat butt in my face, I was deeply regretting it.

"What's going on?" I whispered.

There was a squeak, a thump, and something shattered.

Nugget flipped around and head-butted me hard on the forehead. "We've been standing guard ever since you decided to witch nap. You're lucky to be alive. These dolls are on the attack."

I struggled upright, and my mouth fell open as I took in the scene around the bed. I counted at least thirty destroyed dolls. Their clothing was ripped, their porcelain heads smashed in, and hair was strewn all over the place.

Sitting at the end of my bed were two very proud looking familiars. Russell had what looked like a shredded dress across his shoulders, like a superhero cape.

Nugget jumped up and curled around my neck.

"You dealt with all these dolls while I was asleep?" I said. "You should have woken me. I could have helped."

He wriggled around on my shoulders until he was comfortable and coiled his tail around me. "We figured you needed the rest after the whole Olympus being weird thing."

Hilda scuttled over. She sat on the back of my hand, since her usual place on my shoulder was occupied by Nugget. "I've enjoyed myself. I don't like the dolls' teeth, though. At least two of them had real human teeth in their evil little heads, and they'd been sharpened to points."

I shuddered to think where those teeth had come from. "I appreciate the multiple saves. I owe all of you for this. Breakfast is on me."

"For the next week," Nugget said. "And none of that lousy tinned cat food you keep trying to give me. I keep telling you, I like fresh fish. A lightly poached piece of sea bass in a warm truffle oil will do."

"Dream on. You know I can't cook. But I'll find you something nice in the tinned aisle." My thoughts went to Olympus. I hadn't seen him for the rest of the night. I'd looked around outside for a while, and had expected him to come back, but he didn't show.

There was a guy in serious amounts of pain, and I didn't like to see that. We may have our issues, but he didn't deserve to be hurting. It saddened me that he'd lost his daughter, and I imagined he felt responsible for her disappearance.

Bloom Duke was another name to go on my list of weird things happening in Witch Haven. This darkness had to be stopped.

There was a light tap on the door.

"Uh, oh! I smell a decaying old maid with a dolly obsession and bad manners," Nugget said.

I grimaced as I looked around at the mess. Ursa would throw a fit if she saw this. I dashed over to the door and opened it an inch.

"Oh! Hello." Ursa's top lip curled. "I see you survived the night."

"I'm happy to say, we all did."

"And my dolls were no trouble? I thought they may have played with you a little too roughly." She tried to peer over my shoulder.

"Everything's good." I eased the door closed a fraction. "I was thinking about breakfast, actually. I'm starving after working all night."

"Very well. I suppose you've earned it. Be downstairs in the dining room in ten minutes. Don't expect anything much, though. I never have an appetite first thing."

"Great. Looking forward to it. See you in a few minutes." I shut the door before she could see any shredded dolls and turned back to my familiars. "We have to hide this carnage."

"I don't see why we should," Nugget said. "This is evidence that the dolls are out of control. They should be destroyed. Even the ones that didn't attack us last night. It's only a matter of time before they do something evil."

There were several angry, high-pitched squeaks from the shelves around us.

"He's joking," I said to the dolls.

"No, I'm not," Nugget muttered.

I studied the remaining dolls. I'd hoped they'd quieten down after I destroyed Mary-Sue. I figured she was the conduit toward their mischief making. Perhaps now they'd had a taste of freedom, they'd decided they didn't want to be stuck on a shelf in a soulless room any longer. I couldn't blame them.

"We aren't spending another night stuck in this room," Nugget said. "I need my cat naps. I didn't get any sleep last night."

"And you need your sleep, or you get grumpy," Hilda said.

"We can all catch up on our sleep another time. Let's clear up this mess and then go down and face Ursa." I hunted out a couple of large boxes from another room and stuffed the remains of the destroyed dolls in them.

I placed the boxes back in the room where I found them and piled a load of blankets on top. Ursa would have to understand that there were always losses in every battle, and my familiars were only defending themselves when they destroyed the dolls. Although all the shredded clothing and pulled out hair made it look like they'd had great fun doing it.

I found a bathroom, had a quick freshen up, and then headed down the stairs with my familiars. I walked into the dining room to discover a huge, dark wood antique table that sat twenty people.

Ursa was at the far end at the head of the table. She gestured to the chair to her right.

I headed over and sat down. Nugget took the seat next to me, while Russell perched on the back of the chair, and Hilda clambered onto my shoulder.

I looked at the disappointing piece of pale toast on the plate in front of me and sighed.

"What happened last night? Did you get to the bottom of my doll problem?" Ursa said.

"I thought I had. In fact, I was certain Mary-Sue was behind all this."

"Now you're not so sure? Do you think it could be another one of the dolls?" Ursa took a sip of black coffee. She didn't offer me any, so my mug remained empty.

I pulled apart my toast, gave some to Russell, left a tiny piece on my shoulder for Hilda, and offered Nugget a bit, which he turned his nose up at.

Only when Ursa gave a loud sigh, did I speak.

"I encountered Mary-Sue again last night, and she was full of energy. She was also talking. Has she ever mentioned the name Bloom to you?"

Ursa pursed her lips. "No, I've never heard her say that name. In fact, she's never spoken much before. What did she say to you?"

"She pretended she was a lost child named Bloom. I think she hoped I'd take pity on her and not question her to find out the truth about what turned her evil."

"Mary-Sue's not evil, she's just misunderstood. You must understand that, given the life you've led." Ursa arched an eyebrow.

"A point well made." I set my toast crust down. "I'm interested in who sold you the doll. You said you'd never bought from them before. How did you come to hear about Mary-Sue?"

"I'm on numerous forums and chat groups. We love to collect antique and unusual dolls. A message was posted offering Mary-Sue for sale. Of course, I had to have her. My collection is one of the finest around and she made a wonderful addition to it."

"Until she turned dark and decided to try to kill anyone she came into contact with," I said.

Ursa set her mug down. "Do you think she's hexed? I'd hate to let her go, but the troubles in the house intensified when I moved her in. I tried to contact the person I bought her from, but the message had disappeared, and the messages I sent were returned. Whoever it was, they vanished from the forum."

"Which is suspicious. Could it have been an enemy of yours?" I said. "They posed as a seller and hexed Mary-Sue, knowing she'd cause you problems. Can you think of anyone who'd do that?" I was expecting a long list of names.

"No. I'm well liked, and I'm kind to everyone. I can't think of anyone who'd do such a terrible thing."

Ursa hadn't been all that kind to me. "What about the other collectors who wanted the doll? They must have been angry you got it."

"Collectors may be ambitious, but we're not spiteful. No, I don't have any enemies who'd do this to me."

"So it was bad luck that you bought Mary-Sue?" I shook my head.

"It must have been. This is the first doll I've ever had trouble with." She chewed on her thin slice of dry toast. "What do you propose to do next? If you believe there is a hex on Mary-Sue, can you remove it?"

"I, um, no. That won't be possible." It was far too late for that. There were probably still a few fragments of Mary-Sue left in the fireplace, but that was all. "The best thing to do is get the doll out of the house."

"I don't want her gone. She's a prime collection piece."

"A killer prime collection piece. And it could be impossible to remove the hex. I don't know enough about the magic used on the doll, or who did it. It would take months of trial and error before I figure out a spell to reverse it."

"So what do you suggest I do with her?"

"Get rid of Mary-Sue. Forget you ever met her."

"I can't. She cost too much money to give up on her." Ursa set her hands in her lap. "There must be a way to improve her behavior. I know! I'll perform cleansing rituals on her. That could neutralize the magic."

"You'll need more than a cleansing ritual." I glanced at the door. "I'll deal with her today. You won't ever have to see Mary-Sue again."

"No! She's my doll. I'll try cleansing her and see how that goes. I'm not giving up on her."

I dabbed up toast crumbs on the pad of my finger. It was confession time. "I have bad news. Mary-Sue attacked me last night. I, um, I had to destroy her."

Ursa's eyes bugged wide. "You... killed my precious doll?"

"First off, Mary-Sue can't be killed. She was an object. Admittedly, a horribly hexed object, but she wasn't alive. And secondly, she tried to kill me."

Ursa's bottom lip wobbled. "What did you do to her? I insist on seeing her body."

"Oh, you really don't want to see her. She's in a bad way. You see, Mary-Sue lunged at me. And she was having a bad effect on Olympus. I had to act quickly to destroy the threat."

"Olympus Duke was in my house? I don't allow gentlemen callers in the middle of the night. I hope you and him weren't—"

"No! I have no interest in Olympus. He was just helping me out. He'd been dealing with the gnomes, and once he was finished with them, he offered me a hand with the dolls. Then he started acting weirdly around Mary-Sue, so I had to smash her. There's not much left. She's beyond repair."

"You smashed her!" Ursa shuddered. "You're a terrible witch. You've destroyed an expensive, precious asset."

"To help you! Your life was being ruined because of that malicious doll. She could have killed you in your sleep."

Ursa was silent for a moment, her gaze fixed on her plate. "Was there no other way?"

"Without knowing who hexed her and why, she'd have kept being a problem. I know it's tough to hear, but destroying her was a kindness. Mary-Sue was suffering, too."

Nugget stifled a laugh and hid his face behind my head.

Ursa's expression was glum. "Well, I suppose if this has fixed the problems in my house, that's the price I'll have to accept. But no more damaging my dolls."

I nodded, my thoughts on the ruined heap of dolls I'd woken up to. Something felt wrong about this hexing mystery. If Mary-Sue was the cause of the trouble in this house, then the rest of the dolls shouldn't have bothered us in the night. Should I tell Ursa her problems weren't over and there were more ruined dolls to discover?

No, it was just a residual of the hex stirring things up. The dolls would soon settle. And Ursa had so many of them, she wouldn't miss a few.

Something metallic clattered to the floor outside the dining room.

Ursa jumped out of her seat and stared at the closed door. "Is Olympus still in here?"

"Not that I know of." I hopped up and followed Ursa to the door.

Russell flew behind us, while Nugget remained on my shoulders, and Hilda balanced on my hand.

Ursa yanked open the door and then leaped back, almost knocking into me.

"Eek!" Hilda said.

"Wow! You don't see that every day," Nugget said.

"You sure don't," I whispered.

A life-sized suit of armor, complete with sword waving in its hand, was righting itself from the floor. The visor was up, and two glowing red eyes looked at me.

Ursa slammed the door shut. She turned and glared at me. "You destroyed Mary-Sue. You said that would be an end to my problems. That thing out there should not be moving."

I winced and bit my bottom lip. "Maybe there's more than one problem in your house. After all, it is built on a burial ground."

"That's not an issue. The dead aren't rising and demanding the house be moved. You can't blame your failure on the location of Gravesend Manor."

I wanted to. I doubted very much whether people had been happy about their dearly departed being covered over by this creepy monstrosity.

"Or it could be the residual after-effects of the hex," I said. "I'll keep working on the problem."

Ursa shook her head violently. "No! No more of your lies. You damaged my precious collection of dolls, you destroyed Mary-Sue, and my house is still troubled. You're a charlatan."

I repressed a groan. "I'll figure out why there's a suit of armor running around. It won't get in your way."

A low, clanging bell made me jump. I'd never get used to Ursa's gothic sounding doorbell.

"Now what? A headless horseman, come to take me away?" Ursa yanked open the door again. She dodged past the wobbling suit of armor and marched to the front door.

I waited until the suit of armor had its back to me and ran past with my familiars. I got to the door and saw Storm and Odessa standing outside.

"These two say they're friends of yours," Ursa said, the disdain clear in her voice.

"That's right." I smiled at them.

Ursa sniffed. "I don't like unexpected guests."

"We may be unexpected, but I hope we're welcome." Odessa held up a basket full of muffins. "I've baked my speciality pumpkin spiced muffins. I hope you haven't eaten breakfast yet. They have caramel frosting on top. And chocolate sprinkles."

Ursa lifted her chin and peered into the basket. "I do like your muffins. Very well. Come in, both of you. But keep the noise down. I've already had a trying morning, thanks to your incompetent friend." She took the largest muffin from the basket and walked away. "If you'll excuse me, I have a marauding suit of armor to deal with."

Storm and Odessa both looked at me, curiosity burning in their eyes.

"What are you doing here?" I said. "Not that I'm unhappy to see you. I need rescuing after the night I've had."

"We heard there was a party going down." Storm produced a huge baseball bat from behind her back and swung it in an arc. "Aren't you going to invite us in so we can smash up some dolls?"

Chapter 14

I ushered my friends into Gravesend Manor. "You'd better come in. How did you know I was here?" I closed the door and led them along the hallway.

"People have been whispering about a strange doll possession in Ursa's house. They're saying it's your fault," Storm said.

"We had to come take a look," Odessa said. "And we wanted to make sure you were doing okay after you confronted Olympus. You didn't kill him, did you?"

I tipped back my head. "He's alive. But when will people figure out I'm not the source of evil in this place?"

"No, but you are one of them," Storm said.

I glared at her, but then smiled as I saw the laughter dancing in her eyes.

"Fill us in," Odessa said. "What's happening here? I've heard every possibility from devil dogs through to killer gnomes and everything in between."

"I've yet to meet any devil dogs, but the gnomes are playing up. Olympus was almost their sacrificial victim last night."

Nugget yawned in my ear. "And he would have been, if Indigo hadn't rescued him."

"Wait! What have I missed?" Storm said. "Since when do you rescue the Head of the Magic Council? Last I saw, he wanted you arrested, never to be seen again."

I lifted one shoulder. "We've formed an uneasy alliance. I doubt it'll last long, but he's helping me with the problems in Ursa's house. And he got me out of the Magic Council meeting without losing my power. He even spoke up for me. I was so stunned, I almost fell over."

"You're not the only one who's stunned by that revelation," Storm said. "Why the change of heart?"

"I'm still working that out. Olympus reckons this is just business. Ursa is a problem for the Magic Council, and I could be useful to them."

Odessa's smile was sly. "Oh! I get it. He likes you."

"Nope, that's not it. He had a problem case to deal with, and so stuck it on me."

"I bet that's not all he'd like to stick on you," Storm said.

Odessa snort laughed and thumped her. "Don't be seedy."

"I'm not being seedy. And why not get some action while it's on offer? He might work for a creepoid organization, but he's a gorgeous guy, and he's got influence. You should exploit that."

"I'm not exploiting anyone," I said. "And I'm not here for romance, or action, or anything like that."

"Duck!" Storm swung the bat at my head.

I squeaked, grabbed hold of Nugget so he wouldn't fall off my shoulders, and hit the floor. A few seconds later, porcelain shattered over my head and rained down on me.

I looked up. Odessa stood frozen to the spot, taking in the scene with wide eyes. "Do the dolls all behave like that?"

I scrambled off the floor and nodded, kicking away the fork the doll had been aiming at my head. "Most of them. Even after I destroyed their leader, Mary-Sue."

"What was that noise?" Ursa raced along the hallway, a half-eaten muffin in her hand. She stared at what was left of the attacking doll. "Is that one of my angels scattered across the floor?"

Storm tucked the baseball bat behind her back and looked as innocent as a cherub.

"We're still having a few problems," I said. "It'll calm down soon."

"This is a disgrace. You're looking in the wrong place. My dolls are being used. Such innocence shouldn't be exploited." Ursa knelt on the floor. "Oh, and this was Patti-Jane. She was such a sweet little thing."

"She tried to jump on Indigo and stab her with a dinner fork," Odessa said. "She doesn't seem all that sweet to me."

"Heads up. Incoming!" Storm whirled the bat over her head and smashed two more dolls out of the air.

Ursa yelped and dropped to the floor, while I ducked, and Odessa scurried out of the way.

"Stop your friend!" Ursa said to me. "She's out of control."

"Storm is saving us. You should thank her." I dodged a doll's head as it disengaged from its body thanks to Storm's bat twirling skills. The head slammed into the wall and hit the floor with a thud.

"That's the last of them for now," Storm said.

"You must stop! There has to be some other way to deal with the dolls." Ursa was on her knees, picking up pieces of damaged doll. "I'm sure they can be rehabilitated. They've just gotten a little wild because of this hex."

"Maybe so, but we need to be sure. Russell, Hilda, go scout out the rest of the dolls' movements. Let us know if they're planning any more attacks," I said.

Russell dropped to the floor from his perch on the large clock in the corner of the room. He bobbed his head.

Hilda scrambled onto his back, and they flew off up the stairs.

"While we have a moment's respite from your attacking dolls," I said, "tell me what you've done with my ghost jar."

Ursa glanced at me. "What are you talking about?"

"You saw it when you came to my house," I said. "Why did you steal it?"

She jerked her head back, pulling in her chin so she looked like a startled turtle. "I don't like your tone. I'm not a thief."

"It must have been you. No one else knew my house still existed. You show up, and the next thing I know, the ghost jar is gone."

"I have no use for a ghost jar. Even if I did, I wouldn't take one of yours. They're easy to come by."

Storm tapped the baseball bat against her palm. "The ghost in that jar is important to us. It could have information to help us get Luna back. You wouldn't be holding out on us, would you? I'll do anything to protect my friends."

Ursa staggered to her feet and backed away, her gaze on the baseball bat. "I... I don't know what to say. I'm an upstanding member of the community. I wouldn't steal from you."

"You would if it meant you had one over on Indigo," Storm said. "You were always jealous of Magda. Are you taking out your insecurities by making life difficult for her step-daughter?"

"That's nonsense. I liked Magda. At least, I did until she went on the attack. She was a responsible witch. Which is a lot more than I can say about any of you." Ursa's cheeks were pink. "You burst in here, destroy my dolls, and accuse me of a crime I haven't committed. I have enough stress with my misbehaving dolls and troublesome gnomes. I don't need delinquent witches adding to my concerns."

I glanced at Odessa and Storm. I'd been sneakily poking around to locate the ghost jar and hadn't found it, but I still couldn't decide if Ursa was telling the truth. There wasn't a strong reason she'd take the ghost jar. And they were easy to find or simple enough to create if you needed to catch a spirit.

Something smashed over our heads, and a child-like laughter drifted down the stairs.

"Now look what you've done. My dolls have been upset by your familiars. I must calm them. Don't destroy any more of my angels while I'm not here." Ursa dashed away and up the stairs. "I'm coming, my babies."

"Ursa's super weird around these dolls." Storm ground a doll's head into the carpet under the heel of her boot.

"They're her children," Odessa said. "Ursa doesn't have a family of her own."

"No surprise there. Who'd want to hang out with Ursa for long? Certainly not long enough to get her naked and—"

I shuddered. "You don't need to paint us a picture."

"Ursa must be lonely," Odessa said. "She lives in this huge house on her own and has no friends to speak of, and she only sees her uncle when she has a problem. We should include her in our group. We could have a girls' night and invite her over."

"I'm sure Ursa would prefer to hang out with people her own age," I said.

"Or evil things with porcelain heads and murder on their minds," Storm said.

"She won't want to hang out with us after we've destroyed her doll collection. She's yet to see what happened in her collection room overnight," I said.

Russell zoomed down the stairs, with Hilda on his back.

Hilda dropped onto my hand. "Ursa chased us away. But the dolls didn't follow us. They're more interested in Ursa."

"Is she okay?" I didn't like her, but death by evil dolly wouldn't be a fun experience.

"For now. She's pleading with them to behave. They seem to be listening."

"I know. I'll send her a care package," Odessa said. "That'll put a smile on her face and help her stop worrying about her dolls."

"You can try that," Storm said. "But some people aren't worth saving."

"Everyone's worth saving." Odessa looked around. "I thought you said Olympus was helping you. Where is he?"

"About that. Something odd happened when we were hunting the dolls," I said. "Mary-Sue, the doll in charge, called herself Bloom. She pretended she was Olympus' missing daughter."

Odessa gasped and her hand went to her mouth. "Poor Limpy must have been in bits."

"I had no idea he even had a daughter, or that she was missing," I said. "Do you know what happened?"

"It was so sad," Odessa said. "I met Bloom a few times. Olympus shared custody with his former fiancée, Peony Cashmere. Do you remember her?"

"Sure. She left school at seventeen to set up her own business, didn't she?"

"That's right. She was always so smart. Peony ran an upcycling store. Although she left that all behind years ago. She couldn't bear to be here after what happened to Bloom."

"Olympus told me Bloom went missing when he took her on a job," I said.

"Yes, he was investigating a robbery, although I heard rumors it also involved an illegal death curse. I'd often see him passing through the village with Bloom. She was such a cheerful child. Bright, polite, and such a cutie."

"If you like kids," Storm said.

"Which we do," Odessa said. "Anyway, I heard from Mystica Shade that Olympus went to this house to look at the crime scene. Bloom was supposed to stay outside. There were several members of Magic Council law enforcement around, so he figured she'd be safe. He went inside, and by the time he got back, Bloom was gone."

"She was taken in front of law enforcement?" I said. "That's bold. And odd."

"It was odd, especially since no one remembered seeing Bloom outside," Odessa said. "I'm convinced a memory wipe spell was used. Only three people remember seeing Bloom, and one of them was Olympus. I heard he was beside himself as he tried to find her. He organized a search party, and they looked everywhere."

"It's like she vanished into thin air," Storm said. "It's no surprise. Olympus must have enemies, given the work he does. His past came back to haunt him and took someone he loved."

"That doll saying his daughter's name messed with him," I said. "I didn't know what to do. I destroyed the doll, and he tried to strangle me. He really believed that was his daughter making contact."

"Limpy is still grieving, after all these years. And I know he still looks for her," Odessa said.

"He even tried to hire me to search for Bloom," Storm said. "I told him he was wasting his time. He has way more resources than me."

"Could Peony have taken her?" I said. "Since they're separated, there could have been trouble between them."

"No, it wasn't her. Although that's what Olympus thought to begin with. And Peony was questioned for weeks. And I know her house and the business were searched," Odessa said. "I remember watching as she stood on the sidewalk as the Magic Council took her upcycling place apart. It wasn't long after that, that she talked about leaving. Six months later, she was gone."

"Where is Peony now?" I said.

"I'm not sure," Odessa said.

"The last I heard, she went to a remote magic community and wants nothing to do with Witch Haven." Storm twirled her bat. "It's probably for the best. There are too many tough memories for her to deal with around here."

My heart went out to Olympus and Peony, but I couldn't go getting soft toward him, and I wasn't letting my guard down. He was Magic Council. That was the most important thing in his life.

"Oh! And did you hear the terrible news about Albert?" Odessa said.

"Luna's uncle? No, he's not sick, is he?"

"It's worse than that. He closed the bakery. He said he can't cope. I'm so worried."

I let out a sigh of relief. "You're only worried because you can't get access to his delicious treats."

"It's not just me. Everyone is worried. It's a tragedy. We must find Luna so Albert can be happy again. Witch Haven can't be without its desserts," Odessa said.

Storm laughed and shook her head. "We'll manage, especially with the amount of muffins you bake."

"No! This is serious. My muffins aren't a patch on the bakery goodies."

"What do you suggest we do? Stampede the bakery and insist Albert gets his apron back on?" Storm smirked at me.

Odessa grinned. "I know exactly what we need to do. We combine our powers."

Storm shrugged, and I nodded. It wasn't the first time we'd done that.

"What are you hoping to find if we merge our magic?" I said.

"The secret recipe to Albert's cherry scones?" Storm said.

"Stop it! I'm not that greedy." Odessa jutted out her bottom lip. "I figured we could force the ghost you trapped in the jar to manifest. If Ursa took the ghost jar, the spirit will be close by. It's always easier to force a ghost out of hiding when it's near."

"And if the ghost shows up instantly, it would be proof Ursa took the jar and has been lying to us," I said.

"And then you can get your revenge on her," Storm said.

I considered that option, but payback had already been handed out by the number of dolls that hadn't made it through the night.

"I reckon we can pull this ghost in from anywhere by combining energies. Especially now Indigo is firing on all cylinders," Odessa said.

"I'm firing on something, but this new magic I possess doesn't always react the way I expect it to," I said.

"You don't want to try?" Odessa said.

"No, I'm game. We need to find this ghost."

"Where shall we do the summoning?" Storm said.

"In the dining room. There's an enormous table in there we can use." I led them into the dining room, and we settled at the end of the table.

Hilda sat on my arm, Russell perched on the back of my chair, and Nugget curled himself around my shoulders and looked on with a bored expression on his face.

We'd just linked hands when Ursa bustled into the room, her arms full of dolls. "What are you doing? I didn't say you could use this room. And don't make marks on that table. It's an antique."

"We won't damage the table. We're helping Luna," I said. "And you're welcome to join us. Your energy could strengthen the summoning magic."

"I want nothing to do with your kind of magic," she said.

"Then be useful and fetch us a summoning candle," Storm said.

"What exactly are you summoning? I don't want evilness drawn into this house."

"The ghost you stole from me," I said.

Ursa tutted. "I've already told you, that wasn't me."

"Then prove it by letting us do this summoning," Storm said. "If you're hiding the ghost jar nearby, the ghost inside will appear instantly."

Ursa pursed her lips and narrowed her eyes. "Very well. But you'll fail. That ghost jar isn't in this house."

She marched out of the room, muttering to herself, and returned a moment later, smacking down a large white candle in front of us.

I pressed a finger to the wick, and it ignited. "Thanks. You don't have to watch."

"I do. I'm watching your every move from now on. And so are my dolls. None of them trust you, especially not after you encouraged your bat-wielding friend to cause so much damage." Ursa sat half a dozen dolls on the table in front of us.

"Keep those creepy things away from me," Storm said. "I still have my bat, and I'm happy to use it."

Ursa's face blanched, and she took a step toward her dolls, her hands hovering over them.

"Nugget, keep an eye on the dolls while we summon the ghost," I said.

"If any of them move, I'm taking them out," he said.

Ursa sucked in a breath. But I glared at her, and she didn't say anything.

I centered myself, closed my eyes, and opened my magic.

Storm and Odessa's powers met mine, and they converged across the table, spreading a pale glow around us until it reached the candle.

"There's something here," Odessa said. "I already feel a strong presence. It could be the ghost you trapped."

I nodded. I felt something too, but it didn't feel like either of the ghosts I'd encountered in Luna's apartment. "Let's keep going. It could need help to manifest." I pushed more magic into the summoning.

"I see something forming," Ursa whispered. "Oh! It... can't be. It looks female. It looks like..."

My eyes flicked open. It took me a few seconds to process what I was seeing, but when I did, I was so shocked I forgot how to breathe.

Standing at the other end of the table was Luna's misty, ghostlike form.

Chapter 15

Odessa squeezed my hand as I continued to stare open-mouthed at Luna.

I blinked rapidly to make sure I wasn't dreaming. "Holy broomsticks! Are you both seeing this, or have I officially lost my mind?"

Storm's face was set in a grim expression as she nodded.

Odessa swallowed loudly. "Luna, is that really you?"

Luna floated closer, drifting through several chairs until she reached us. She smiled. "Wow! That was quite a ride. I've never been summoned before. You awesome ladies have power."

Disbelief made my heart race. "But... but you can't be here. Not like this."

Luna tilted her head as her attention fixed to me. "Don't be sad. I'm at peace. I have no problems now, and the ghosts have stopped bothering me. I have you to thank for that."

I shook my head so hard my ears rang. "No! You're not real. You can't be a..." I couldn't even say the word ghost.

"Let's all take a breath," Odessa said. "We need to figure out what's going on. Luna, where are you?"

Luna spread her arms out. "I'm free. I feel no pain. I've moved on."

"Where have you moved to?" Storm said. "We were trying to summon the spirit Indigo trapped in her ghost jar. The one from your apartment. We didn't expect to summon you."

Luna laughed. "I'm still getting used to my new situation. Everything happened so fast. I'm not sure where I am, but it feels safe. It doesn't feel like I have anything to worry about. Which means none of you need to worry either."

"Of course, we're going to worry." My voice was hoarse because my throat was so tight with emotion. "You got taken from the hospital while you were sick. And now this. Do you remember what happened to you?"

She drifted slowly from side to side. "I... I don't remember that. I remember you coming back to Witch Haven, and me asking for your help. I remember the ghost causing trouble. I got sick because it attached itself to me. Then I felt better. After that, it's a blur."

"Who killed you?" Storm said. "Tell us who took you from the hospital, and we'll make them pay."

"No! No one's getting hurt. There's no need. Not when I'm so happy."

"You can't be happy. You're dead!" I said.

Odessa had tears in her eyes, and even Storm looked on the verge of crying.

I was still too shocked to process all of this. I'd failed Luna. I was supposed to help her with her ghost problem and give her her life back. Instead, I'd contributed to her death. This was the worst possible outcome.

"Please, don't be unhappy," Luna said. "You're my closest friends and I love you all dearly, but I don't need your help anymore. In fact, I'm here to help you."

"You want to help us?" I said. "With what?"

"I heard you summoning a ghost, so I came to see if I could assist. Now I'm one of the ghostly gang, I can easily speak to other spirits. I don't even need to use my magic to do it."

"Luna, I'm so sorry. I messed up. You weren't supposed to die," I said.

"Oh, Indigo. This isn't your fault. Accidents happen."

"Your death was an accident?" Odessa said.

Luna floated about for a few seconds. "I don't know. It may have been."

"If that ghost killed you, I won't rest until it's punished," I said.

"No! Don't go revenge ghost hunting," Luna said. "You don't want any more deaths on your conscience."

I hung my head in shame. "You can't kill a ghost."

"True, but your dark days are over. You're a good witch. That's enough revenge talk. Besides, I want to be useful. And helping you is the least I can do. After all, you risked everything when you stayed in Witch Haven to solve my problems."

"Which I've epically failed to do," I said. "Luna, is this really happening? Somebody pinch me. I need to wake up from this nightmare."

"We all do," Odessa said. "But I think it is happening. Luna, are you sure there's nothing we can do for you?"

"No, and it's my turn to be of service to you. I can sense a mysterious presence in this house. I can take it away if that's the problem."

"Yes! It must be the problem I've been struggling with. Do that," Ursa said. "I want my house returned to normal, which is something your useless friends have failed to help me with."

"No! Stay here, Luna. We need to find out what happened to you," I said. "Don't you care that you're dead?"

Luna nodded at Ursa as if she hadn't heard me. "It would be my pleasure to free this house from one of its many burdens."

"Many burdens?" Ursa scowled. "This house isn't burdened."

"I disagree." Luna patted a head of one of the dolls sitting on the table. "You have such pretty dolls. Evil, but pretty."

Ursa stared at her dolls. "Thank you, I think. Your friends don't have such good taste."

"Oh, my friends all have great taste," Luna said. "Now, give me a minute to look around. I'll find the source of your latest trouble and deal with it."

I shared a stunned look with Odessa and Storm. This was too weird. Why didn't Luna care how she died?

"Luna, we really need to talk about this," Odessa said.

"I'll be back in two shakes of a broomstick." Luna vanished.

"Hello, is there anyone here?"

"Who's that interrupting?" Ursa turned to the door.

"It sounds like Albert," I said.

Ursa hurried to the dining room door and pulled it open.

Albert Black stumbled through the doorway, his eyes wide, and his thinning hair sticking up on his head. "Oh, I'm so glad I found you. I heard you might be here." He nodded at Ursa, but his attention was on me. "Forgive the intrusion, but I had to find you, Indigo. I've got news about Luna."

I glanced at my friends, guilt racing through me. "So have I. And it's not good news."

"Oh! My news is excellent. I know what happened to her." He hurried to the table and leaned his hands flat on it as he caught his breath.

"You do?" I looked around for any sign of Luna's ghost returning, but she had yet to make a reappearance.

He nodded. "Yes! She's dead."

My mouth opened, but I didn't know what to say.

Odessa took charge. She pushed back her seat and hurried to Albert. "Yes, she seems to have left us. I'm so sorry for your loss."

He smiled. "It's fine."

"Are you really okay?" I said. Luna had been his only family, and it was no secret how much he'd been struggling since she disappeared.

Albert nodded. "It's good news, like I said. It means—"

Ursa gasped and her hand went to her chest. "Did you all feel that? The hex has been lifted. It suddenly feels much lighter in here. Luna must have neutralized the magic."

Albert looked around, his expression bemused. "Luna is here?"

"Possibly. We're still figuring out that mystery," I said. "How did you learn about what happened to Luna?"

He rubbed his chin. "She told me."

Ursa bustled to the table. "Luna's done it. I never thought much of Miss Grimstone, she always had her head in the clouds and her baked goods were often questionable, but she's succeeded when you all failed."

"It looks like it. But if Luna fixed your hex, she'd have come back and told us," I said.

"Why? She's not bothered with you anymore. Luna has a new life. Well, a new death to explore." Ursa brushed away my comment with a hand.

"She wouldn't have left without saying goodbye to us." I stared around the room, hoping to see Luna. I had so many questions for her. "We need to know how she died."

"And if anyone had anything to do with it," Storm said.

Albert chuckled. "Forget all about that. Everything is fine now. There's no need to worry."

He sounded just like Luna, waving away concerns about her death.

Ursa scooped up the dolls from the table. "Luna is my fairy godmother. She's finally helped this house find peace."

Albert nodded, a smile on his face. "She always was a good girl. She liked helping other people and had a kind heart."

"Albert, if you don't mind me saying, you don't seem sad that Luna is no longer with us," I said.

"Why should I be sad? I know the truth. I don't need to wonder about what happened to her," he said.

Ursa walked to the door. "Indigo, your work here is done. It's time you all left."

"No. We should stay. Luna will come back," I said.

"Luna has done what she needed to for me. She discovered the hex and removed it." Ursa arched her thin eyebrows. "Out you go. I've had enough of witches cluttering my home and making unacceptable demands."

"I don't want to leave until we learn that Luna's okay," I said. "I mean, of course, she's not. After all, she's dead." I was still struggling to get my head around this.

Ursa walked over and snuffed out the candle with her fingers. "You've overstayed your welcome. And I have a mess to clean up." She glared at Storm.

I looked at Odessa and Storm. This felt horribly wrong. Had we really just seen Luna, or was something playing tricks on us?

I stood and walked around the room. The house did feel different. The oppressive, stuffy atmosphere was gone, and the whole place seemed less tense.

"What do you reckon, Nugget?" I stared out the window. "Is this case closed? Is my best friend really dead?"

"All I know is something weird happened here. I can't tell you what, but even the stuffed animals staring at us from the corner seem more relaxed. Maybe Luna did come to see us. It could have been her way of saying goodbye. She helped you out one last time."

I sniffed back tears. It still felt wrong to me.

"Everybody out," Ursa said. "And I shall be telling the Magic Council about this."

I turned from the window. "What will you tell them?"

"The truth. The job was completed."

I glanced at the others. "So... you're happy?"

"Not particularly. There were plenty of problems."

"You have nothing to complain about," Storm said. "The hex has gone. The methods used may have been unusual, but the outcome was what you wanted."

"That's true enough." Ursa walked to a side cabinet and pulled open a drawer, then headed over to me and handed me an envelope.

"What's this?" I didn't take the envelope.

"Your payment."

"Payment!" I grabbed the envelope and opened it. It was stuffed full of cash. I had no idea I'd get paid for this job. I'd only done it because Olympus forced my hand.

"I've taken out twenty-five percent of the final fee so I can replace my destroyed dolls," Ursa said. "I'm sure Olympus will understand. Make sure he gets it."

"Um, Thanks. Do you need a receipt, or something?"

"No. Now, no more dawdling." Ursa shooed us out of the dining room.

Storm and Odessa walked either side of Albert, while he waved his hands around and talked. He was being far too animated and excited for someone who'd just learned a family member was dead.

The front door opened by itself, and we hurried outside.

"You don't want to linger out there," Ursa said from the doorway. "The gnomes don't like people lurking around." She shut the door.

I stared at it for a second and shook my head, then turned to Albert. He was crying, but also had a huge smile on his face.

I walked over and caught hold of his hand. "You must be in shock."

"I... really can't tell you how I feel." He gripped my hand. "Good, I think."

"Tell me more about how Luna came to you."

"She came through to me while I was in the bakery. I thought I was imagining it at first, but she appeared in the kitchen and told me not to worry about her."

"Let's get out of here." Storm was staring at the foliage, her bat held out in front of her. "We're being watched by something that doesn't feel friendly."

"Good idea." I hurried the group away from the house and out through the gates.

"Albert, what did Luna tell you when she appeared?" Odessa said.

"She said she'd left Witch Haven and then died."

"How did she die?" I said.

"I don't know."

"And Luna just left the hospital voluntarily?" I said.

"She must have done." He rubbed his hands together as if he was cold. "I was worrying about nothing."

"You weren't. We all saw Luna when she was sick. You don't recover from something like that overnight, even if you have powerful healing spells being blasted into you," I said. "Are you sure she mentioned nothing about how she died?"

"All Luna said was that she was happy, safe, and not to worry. And I'm not worrying. I know what happened now. I can move on with my life."

"How? You only know half the story," I said. "Aren't you curious to know why Luna left Witch Haven? Or how she died? What if her death wasn't an accident? There could be a killer out there."

"Luna would have said if something bad happened to her. I trust my Luna. She was a good girl and always wanted to do the right thing. That's why she came back as soon as she could. She knew I'd be troubled about her disappearance."

This was making no sense.

"I have an excellent idea. You must come back to the bakery with me," Albert said.

"That's sweet of you, but you must need time to process this sad news," Odessa said.

"I already have. And I want to celebrate."

"What have you got to celebrate?" I said.

"Knowing that my wonderful niece is content. You must come back with me. It'll be a reward for your hard work. And I imagine you've missed my baking, Odessa."

Odessa blushed. "I have, but you don't want the stress of us being around."

He patted her arm. "The three of you were close to Luna. She'd want this. And you did so much to help her."

I rubbed my forehead. I hadn't done enough. I'd only thought Luna was missing. I didn't think for one second her ghost would suddenly appear and tell us all was right with the world.

"I'll go on ahead and open up. Anything you desire, it's all yours." Albert raced off at a jaunty jog, whistling loudly.

"That was super weird," Storm said. "Does anyone else think Albert's not behaving like himself?"

I raised my hand, and so did Odessa.

"It's a front," Odessa said. "He's putting on a brave face because he doesn't want us to be concerned about him. Men can be like that. They don't enjoy opening up about their feelings."

"He's failed. I'm doubly concerned about him," I said. "How did Luna appear so easily? We weren't even summoning her. I wasn't thinking about her. I wanted to talk to the ghost from her apartment."

"Maybe she came through because they had a connection," Odessa said. "That ghost attached itself to Luna. When we summoned it, we brought through Luna instead."

"I think we should stay close to Albert for now," I said. "There's something off about this whole setup."

"I'm happy to stick around, so long as he feeds us," Storm said.

"Let's catch up with him. I don't want to leave him on his own, in case he has a breakdown all over the cream pies," I said.

We raced after Albert, but he was surprisingly fast on his feet and was already inside the bakery, pulling out trays of cakes, pastries, and brownies as we entered.

He waved us over to the counter. "Take a look at what I've got for you. And I expect you all want hot chocolate with whipped cream on top. Luna loved that."

"Hot chocolate would be great. But we can help make that," Odessa said.

"No, you're my guests. I already have a batch brewing. And you're not paying for a thing. Go sit down and I'll bring over a tray of treats for you to sample." Albert walked to the door and flipped the closed sign to open. "And while I'm here, I may as well get things back on track. There's no point in denying my customers any longer than necessary."

Odessa seemed determined to offer her help, but Albert was already striding to the door. I tugged her to a table with Storm and we sat down.

"I have so many questions, I don't know where to start," I said.

"Same here. It makes no sense, Luna's ghost just appearing to us," Storm said. "Was that really her?"

"It looked like her," Odessa said. "And it sounded like her. But I'm sure she wouldn't be so calm if she woke up dead."

"And Luna avoided our questions," I said. "She wouldn't reveal how she died. She ignored me when I quizzed her. That's not like Luna."

"Some ghosts never remember their moment of death," Odessa said. "So that's not so strange."

"Luna would be freaking out if she got turned into a ghost. It's not her time to die. This is all wrong," I said.

"What are you thinking?" Storm said.

I waited until Albert had delivered a tray of delicious cakes and hot chocolate before answering. "We're being deceived."

"By who?" Odessa mumbled around a mouthful of triple chocolate brownie.

"Or what?" Storm said.

I took a long drink of my hot chocolate and wiped my whipped cream mustache away with the back of my hand. "I don't know. Something that doesn't want us to keep investigating what happened to Luna."

Odessa leaned across the table. "Could it be the darkness? Have the troubles reached Luna?"

"And now it's messing with us," Storm said. "But why do that? What purpose does it have in sending a ghost that looks like Luna to talk to us?"

"To throw us off its scent," I said. "We've been poking around to see what we can find out about Luna and the ghosts bothering her. That could have stirred something up. Maybe we got too close to the truth, so needed to be distracted. And what's more distracting than your best friend vanishing and then showing up as a ghost?" I shuddered and drank more hot chocolate.

Storm nodded. She grabbed a cherry pie and took a huge bite.

I hovered a hand over the tray and chose a chocolate orange truffle cake. I took a bite. "And then there's Albert. Why isn't he devastated? He was almost dancing with joy as we walked back here. Luna was his life. He loved nothing more than to make her happy, yet he's acting like it's a relief to find her dead."

"Maybe he's another victim of this darkness," Storm said.

"Um, Indigo. We have a problem." Odessa stuffed the rest of her brownie into her mouth and pointed over my shoulder.

I turned and gulped. There were half a dozen customers in the bakery, and they were glaring at me. I'd been so focused on the shocking discovery about Luna, that I'd forgotten I was top of the most wanted list in Witch Haven. I hadn't even thought that coming into the bakery was a dumb idea. It was an idea I now regretted.

"Grab the food, we can get out the back way," Storm said.

"It's too late for that." Odessa pointed at the back door that led to the kitchen, the toilets, and the alleyway. Two stern-faced guys stood there with their arms crossed over their chests and magic sparking on their fingers.

Albert seemed unaware of the growing tension in the bakery as he placed cakes in boxes and rang up a sale. He was laughing and whistling to himself.

"Hey, Albert. We could do with some help over here," I said.

He looked up and laughed. "You're fine. You're exactly where you need to be. Eat up."

My stomach gurgled and my head grew heavy. I staggered to my feet. "Does anyone else feel weird?"

"I feel fine," Nugget said. "But then I haven't been gorging myself on sugar."

"I don't think it's that."

Odessa gripped her stomach and winced. "Now you mention it, I don't feel so good."

I staggered forward, trying to get to the door, but was pushed back by a customer.

"I just want to leave. I need some fresh air." I tried to get past the woman, but she shoved me back, this time harder.

Nugget hissed at the woman.

"You're not going anywhere, witch. It's time you paid for what you did," she said.

The rest of the customers around her murmured their agreement.

I tried to object as my knees gave out. I sank to the cold tiled floor, the room spinning and my stomach turning over.

Hilda scuttled along beside me, while Russell flew overhead, cawing his distress as I crawled back to the others and grabbed the edge of the table. My hand hit the tray with the food on.

Oh, crud! The cakes and the hot chocolate. Had Albert put something in them to weaken us?

A bitter taste flooded my mouth, and I fought nausea.

I shuffled around to see the others. Storm was slumped down, not moving, and Odessa's face was contorted in pain as she gripped her stomach and groaned.

I looked at Albert as black dots appeared in my vision. "What did you do?"

Chapter 16

Wood smoke filled my nose as I slowly resurfaced back to consciousness. I was outside, lying on my back, and it was dark.

I took a deep breath. There must be a fire burning nearby, because the air was smoky and burned down my throat as I swallowed.

I blinked several times, trying to figure out exactly where I was.

The last thing I remembered was being in Albert's bakery, eating cake and talking to Storm and Odessa about Luna's ghost.

The cake and the hot chocolate! Of course. Albert did something bad to us. But why? Had Luna's death driven him insane?

"She's awake," someone shouted.

I peered into the gloom and tensed as a crowd of villagers appeared. None of them looked happy to see me. What were they doing?

My head wouldn't stop spinning, and my limbs felt like they were made of stone. I could barely move. Whatever magic Albert had performed on me had left me weak. I was never buying another cake from him again.

"Get her on top of the pyre," a guy yelled.

I scrunched my brow. What was he talking about? He couldn't mean... I turned my head and groaned. To my right was a huge pile of wood. Stuck in the middle was a pole. You didn't need to be a genius to work out that I was about to be tied to that pole. These villagers planned to have themselves a little witch burning.

Two huge guys I didn't recognize grabbed my arms and dragged me to the pyre. They hauled me up and tied me against the pole. I was too weak to resist and didn't even try to struggle.

"You're making a mistake," I said. "You don't have to do this."

They both grunted and hurried away.

"Indigo Ash. You're a dangerous witch. It's time your reign of terror ended."

I recognized that voice. It was Cornelia Norwood, the owner of the local inn. The last time I'd seen her, she'd been in her late thirties and a real vixen.

The same couldn't be said for her now as I picked her out from the crowd. She had on an eye patch, and a messy scar ran down one side of her face. A scarf covered her once striking amber hair.

I grimaced and looked away. I knew exactly where she got those injuries from. "Cornelia, you have to listen to me. I'm innocent. Whatever you think I did, I didn't do it."

"You're telling me you didn't help to murder sixty-six people in this village?" Cornelia pointed at her scarred face. "You didn't do this to me? You didn't try to burn down my business and ruin my life?"

I struggled against the bindings, but they were too tight, and my brain was too confused to try a spell to help get me free. "Yes, but I've paid for those crimes. I was in prison for a long time, and then in rehabilitation. I'm not here to cause trouble. I'm trying to help Luna Grimstone."

"You're not helping. You took her." An old woman with a hunched back pointed a finger at me. "We all know you're behind this. You're behind the problems in this village."

"I'm not. I'll hold my hands up to what I did when I was younger, but all the other stuff has nothing to do with me. There's a problem in Witch Haven, and I'm figuring out what that is. I plan to stop it."

"So do we," Cornelia said. "And we can do that by getting rid of you."

"You killed my mom," a woman in her late twenties yelled at me. "And you laughed while you did it."

"And you burned down my house," a guy shouted. "I had everything taken from me because of you."

The crowd continued to hurl accusations at me until tears clouded my vision and my chin dropped to my chest. They were right. I was a killer. Maybe I deserved to die. Prison wasn't enough for someone like me. If I could be controlled by dark magic once, it would be easy for it to catch me again. And what's to say the next time I wouldn't stop? I'd kill everyone in my path.

Since coming back here, I'd tried so hard to be normal and accepted. But the truth was, I wasn't. I was weak. I'd let the darkness consume me, and innocent people had been hurt.

Albert bounded over, a smile on his face. "Hi, Indigo." He waved at me.

"Albert, help me. Make everyone else see sense. I've been trying to help Luna. You know that."

He nodded and then turned to Cornelia. "She must die. Can I be the first to light the fire?"

"Albert, wait! You're not yourself. You don't want me dead."

"There's nothing wrong with me. But I've not felt happy in a long time," he said. "Now we've captured you. Finally, the village can get some peace."

"What about Luna? Why aren't you sad about losing her?"

"Oh, I am. I'm devastated by my loss, but your death will make up for that. I demand vengeance. A life for a life. Although Luna was worth twenty of you, and she didn't deserve to die."

"I agree. She was an amazing friend. I'd trade my life for hers in a heartbeat if it brought her back. And I want to find out what happened to her." I squirmed in the bindings, my head slowly becoming less woozy. "Albert, listen to me. I'm not convinced Luna is dead. The ghost we saw, maybe it wasn't her."

"It was. It looked just like her."

"But it didn't act like her. Luna would never have behaved that way. Sure, she'd have wanted to make sure we were doing well and wouldn't miss her too much, but she wouldn't have taken her sudden death so lightly. She'd have wanted to know what happened to her."

"You can't claim to know Luna. You've not been around for over a decade." Albert turned to the watching crowd. "And we all know why that is."

They all grumbled an agreement.

"Don't you want to lay her to rest?" I said. "You don't even know where Luna's body is. You can't get closure until you find her. I'll help with that."

"No, all I want is for you to die. It's what you deserve. You killed my Luna."

"No, I didn't. And if you'd listen, you'd realize I was making sense. That ghost wasn't Luna. She could still be alive. We have to find her. Albert, let me go."

Albert ignored me and danced around the fire, waving his arms and laughing.

Some of the other villagers joined him, while the rest stood in front of me and continued to yell insults.

I narrowed my eyes and stared into the darkness. A red mist was creeping through the crowd. I couldn't see it unless I blurred my vision slightly, but it was there. Was this the darkness taking over? Could this be the work of the witch coven that wanted control of the village? They were here and slowly infecting everyone with hatred and fear so they'd be easy to manipulate.

"Burn the witch! Burn the witch!" The chant grew all around me as more and more villagers joined in.

My head was slowly clearing, and magic sparked on my fingertips. I could blast my way out of here, but if I did, people could get hurt, and I wanted no more deaths on my conscience.

There had to be a non-lethal way I could escape. I looked around, trying to find a friendly face, but all I saw was anger. There was no-one here to help me. And there was no sign of Odessa, Storm, or my familiars. What had happened to them?

"Albert, since you've been recently wronged by this terrible witch, you may have the honor of lighting the witch pyre once we have completed our rituals." Cornelia walked to a metal can. She pulled out a long stick and sparked a flame on the end, before handing it to Albert.

"I won't let you down." Albert took the burning stick and bowed, before turning to me. "We will cast you and your evilness out of Witch Haven for good."

A part of me wanted to scream and blow this place to smithereens, but I also knew I deserved this. Perhaps this was my fate finally coming full circle. No one should get away with killing so many people. How could I expect anything other than long held hatred and resentment bubbling in this village?

Maybe that's what all the problems people were facing were about. They couldn't forget the crimes I'd committed. With me gone, it would give them peace so they could move on. My death would make them happy.

"Bring out the others," Cornelia said. "I want this witch to see the true impact of her behavior. She must suffer."

"The others?" My head shot up as the crowd parted.

Storm, Odessa, and my familiars were carried out by a group of villagers. They were thrown down at the bottom of the pyre.

Cornelia stood over them, a wicked smile on her face. "We plan to kill your accomplices and smite out all the evil in one go."

Horror struck me like a spiked sledgehammer as I stared at my friends and familiars unconscious on the ground. The people I most cared about were at risk. And I really did care for all of them. I wanted my life back in Witch Haven more than anything. I needed to be surrounded by my friends and my familiars and have the chance to help others. There was no way I was going to lose that.

"Get them on the pyre," Cornelia said. "We'll burn them all at once."

"They're not involved." Panic made my heart ricochet in my chest. "I take the blame for everything. Let them go."

"They're not innocent. We know you've been spending time with Storm and Odessa," Cornelia said. "You may think you've been clever, hiding as you infect us with your magic, but we've grown wise to your dark ways. You fooled us once, but you won't do it again. Everyone you've associated with since you returned must be destroyed."

"But not me," Albert said, his sunny disposition faltering. "I was tricked by her, too."

Cornelia patted his arm. "Of course not. You've had a great grievance done to you by Indigo. We'll set that right. Luna's murder will be avenged."

I struggled in my bindings as Storm and Odessa were tied to the pole. An unconscious Hilda was placed on my left shoulder, Russell was tucked inside my jacket, and Nugget hung around my neck.

I nudged Hilda with my chin to get her to wake, but she didn't move. I did the same with Nugget, wincing as I saw a deep gash on his head. His claws were also shredded, suggesting he hadn't gone down quietly.

I may be guilty, but none of them were. It was my fault they were in this mess, and it stopped now.

Albert did another staggering dance around the pyre, growing closer as he dabbed at the wood beneath my feet and laughing as it began to smoke.

I grabbed Odessa's arm and squeezed. "Wake up! We're in trouble."

Odessa didn't stir.

I tried to reach Storm, but she was tied with her back to me, so I couldn't even see her.

The amethyst necklace I wore heated against my skin. My magic was ready to flare out and protect me, and I wasn't sure how much control I'd have over it.

"Everyone get back!" I yelled. "You're in danger."

The crowd ignored me as they encouraged Albert to start the fire.

I tried to calm my speeding heart. If my emotions got any more out of control, my magic would become unstable, and then I'd do people real damage.

I repeated my calls for people to get out of the way, but it was as if they couldn't hear me. They were so fueled by their bloodlust, and all they wanted to see was me burned to a crisp.

An air of defeat sunk over me as the smoke intensified. I was about to lose everything, and I'd only just gotten it all back. I had my amazing friends, my familiars, and a home I loved. Now it was being taken. I'd had a glimpse of something amazing, but who was I kidding? I was a broken witch. I deserved to be stuck on top of this pyre.

But my friends didn't. There had to be a way I could help them get free.

"Begin the fire ritual," Cornelia said.

Albert halted from stabbing at the wood. "Can't we just burn her?"

"We will. But we must observe the proper rituals. Everyone join hands and we'll offer this witch and her accomplices to the darkness. It will take them and leave this place. The flames can consume what's left."

Albert glared at Cornelia. The lit stick he held dangled dangerously close to the wood beneath my feet, and embers dropped onto the pyre.

"Albert, join with me." Cornelia held out her hand. "We must do this right."

"There's nothing right about burning witches," I said. "Don't you know your witch history?"

Albert laughed at me, then danced over to Cornelia and grabbed her hand.

A groan had me jerking my head around. Odessa was finally stirring.

"Hey! Wake up. We're about to be flambéed," I whispered.

Odessa flopped her head around, her eyes fluttering open. "Urgh! I feel terrible. What's going on?"

"We're about to go up in flames."

"Huh? Is that what I can smell? Are we on fire?" She shook her head and looked around. "What are we doing up here?"

"The villagers have revolted. And I think Albert put something in our drinks to make us pass out so they could bring us here."

"He wouldn't..." her words died as she continued to look around. "Is this a witch pyre?"

"Yep. And we're the main attraction."

"Ooooh! This is bad," Odessa said. "But Albert would never drug us."

"He must be sick. This is all my fault. No one else should be up here. I deserve this, but you and Storm don't. I tried to reason with the villagers to get them to let you go, but—"

"What are you talking about? You don't deserve to be burned at the stake." Odessa wriggled beside me until her fingers wrapped around my arm. "Why would you say that?"

"Because of what happened when I helped kill all those people, coming back here to deal with Magda's house, and then everything going wrong with Luna. I'm responsible. Let the villagers burn me. It might make them happy."

Odessa dug her nails into my arm. "You hang on just a minute. Indigo, you're a good witch. I've always trusted you. Your magic is the strongest and most powerful I've ever felt. You've got good running through you."

"I did until my goodness was corrupted. I'm not such a good witch, anymore. What if it happens again? The villagers are right. Get rid of me and solve the problem."

"You must have had a knock to the head if that's what you truly believe," she said. "It's the village that's dark. Feel it!"

"What am I supposed to feel, other than abnormally warm feet?" The fire ritual was still going on, but the wood was already smoking. It would only be a few minutes before the fire ignited.

"You're still not using your magic properly. Reach out and touch what's around us. I've only got half my wits about me thanks to Albert's drugging spell, and I can still sense it in the air. Tune out the noise and use your senses. What does your magic tell you?"

"Do you mean the red mist that's seeping through the crowd?"

"Yes! If that's how you see the problem. I smell moldy cheese." She gave a tiny shrug. "I sometimes smell magic better than I see it."

I blocked out the chants from the villagers as best I could and closed my eyes. After a few seconds, a heavy, sticky sensation engulfed me. It tickled my nose and made me want to sneeze. It also aroused my anger and made me want to lash out. If everyone in Witch Haven felt like this, no wonder things were out of control.

I opened my eyes and stared at Odessa.

"Do you get it now?" she said. "Something's horribly wrong with Witch Haven. Everyone's denied it for too long, but we can't anymore. And it's not because you've come back."

I nodded. I did get it. There was a twisted, creepy vibe running through this place. This was bigger than Luna and her ghost problem, and it was more complicated than Ursa and her hexed dolls. And whether or not I'd caused this, I had to set things right. But there was no way I could do that once I'd become barbecued.

"We're getting off this witch pyre," I said. "It's time to give this village a shake up and get everyone to see sense. Are you with me? It won't be easy. The villagers aren't your fans now they know we're friends again."

"I don't give two hoots about what the villagers think about our friendship," Odessa said. "I'll back you all the way."

I grinned at her. "Then let's wake everyone up and get out of here, before we become dry roasted witches."

Chapter 17

"Storm's still not awake," Odessa said. "She ate the biggest piece of cherry pie, so could have received a bigger hit of the magic Albert dosed us with."

"Blast her with a spell," I said. "Something to make her tingle and get the blood pumping."

"An ice blast will do the trick. She hates being cold. She bitches like a summer elf every time the temperature drops below sixty."

While Odessa worked her magic on Storm, I kept a close eye on the villagers as they came to the end of their fire ritual.

I couldn't reach Russell with my hands tied, though I jiggled about to see if I could get him to stir.

Nugget, however, was within reaching distance of my mouth. He'd hate me for doing this, but I caught his tail between my teeth and bit him.

He stiffened and then shrieked. He leaped in the air and landed belly down on my head.

Nugget hissed in my ear, and his claws dug into my scalp. "Did you just bite me?"

"Sorry, but I had to get your attention. Take a look around. We're in trouble."

He hissed again, and his head swiveled to the chanting crowd. "Is this some kind of horrible nightmare? They want to burn us?"

"They do. But we're not letting that happen. Try to rouse Hilda. I can't get her awake."

Nugget growled low in his chest, then hopped onto my shoulder and licked Hilda's head.

There was a yelp from behind me and lots of cursing. Storm was awake.

"Why do I have an icicle hanging off my nose?" she growled out.

"It worked!" Odessa said. "I knew you'd wake up when you got cold enough."

"What the heck is going on?" Storm said. "I can't see anything. What's with all the chanting?"

"Long story short. Albert drugged us, and the whole village has turned out to see us burn on top of a witch pyre," I said.

Storm groaned. "I knew I shouldn't have gotten out of bed this morning. Odessa, if you don't get this icicle off my nose, you'll be in a world of pain."

"We'll all be in a world of pain soon," I said. "The villagers have just finished their ritual. Now it's time for the burning." I watched with wide eyes as Albert emerged from the crowd, holding aloft the burning stick.

"Do you have any last words?" he said.

"I absolutely do. And I want all of you to listen." I raised my voice and added a little magic boom for effect so no one would miss what I was about to say. "I'm not the danger in Witch Haven. I haven't been back here for long, so I don't know about all the problems you've faced, but I've heard about many of them. This place is troubled. And I know where the trouble is coming from."

"It's coming from you," someone yelled.

"No, it's not. There's a dark witch coven that wants to take control of Witch Haven. They gave Magda Ash tainted magic and threatened my life. They said if she didn't do what they told her to, I'd die. Magda was trying to protect me. She believed the magic she used on you wouldn't kill anyone. The witch coven lied to her."

"Just like you're lying to us now," the woman with a hunched back said. "You're trying to save yourself and your friends."

"No, I know what I did was wrong. And if it was only me on top of this witch pyre, I'd let you do whatever you wanted to me. But you're trying to hurt people I love, and that's wrong. I can't let that happen."

"We lost people we cared about because of you," Cornelia said. "You should feel the same loss. Maybe then you'd understand the mess you left behind."

"I do. I lost Magda that day. I lost her to the darkness the witch coven gave her. She was only trying to protect her family. She didn't know she'd lose control, or that the magic would infect me. Neither of us had any idea the damage it would do. But now it's here, and we need to face the danger together. If we unite, we can defeat this darkness. You must all feel it. This is what's making life in Witch Haven so hard."

The crowd went quiet, then people began to talk to their neighbors. Were they understanding there could be a different way of doing things?

"Enough of this," Cornelia said. "We'll all feel better once you're dead. Albert, light the fire."

Russell shuffled around inside my jacket and let out a hoarse caw, as if he had a sore throat.

There was a cheer as Albert thrust the lit stick into the pyre.

"They won't listen to us," Odessa said. "And I refuse to go down in flames."

"I'm with you there," I said. "Can you reach around far enough to grab Storm? We'll join magic and get out of here."

"Yes! I've got her," Odessa said.

"How's Hilda doing, Nugget?" I said.

"She's faking being unconscious. I think she enjoys getting a tongue bath from me."

"I'm not faking anything," Hilda muttered. "It's just taking me a while to get the feeling back in my legs."

I let out a sigh of relief. My familiars were all awake. They'd be okay. Now, if we could break out of this spell holding us, we'd have a chance to get free and escape the growing flames.

The amethyst necklace glowed hot on my skin again. I had to trust my magic. I was so used to being fearful of it, that I still doubted my powers. But I had my friends beside me and my familiars on hand. I could do this. We could do this together.

Odessa gripped my fingers. "Are you ready?"

"Yep," I said. "Storm, is everything good with you?"

"Heck, yes. Get me out of here."

"Hold on to Hilda, Nugget," I said. "I don't want any of you falling into the flames."

I blocked out the crowd noise again and concentrated on channeling my magic into Odessa and Storm. My magic knew them. It liked them. Over the years we'd grown up together, our powers had often mingled. They melded perfectly as a hot wave of energy flooded out, breaking the binding spells holding us in place.

I shook out my arms and turned to Odessa and Storm, making sure to clutch Russell close so he didn't slip out of my jacket. "Are you both good?"

"Other than being a bit sweaty and gross, I'm fine," Odessa said. She thrust out her hands and doused the flames flickering toward us.

The crowd watching us gasped, and several people backed away, the anger on their faces turning to fear.

"No one dies," I said to Storm and Odessa. "Everyone isn't acting themselves. We have to make allowances for that."

"I'm not so sure about that. There are a few heads out there I'd like to crack wide open." Storm glowered at the watching crowd.

"No! They're not responsible for their actions. We need to help them, not hurt them," I said.

"Get her," Cornelia yelled. "Don't let the witches get away. They have to pay for what they've done."

"You're sure about not hurting anyone?" Storm said. "I've never liked Cornelia much."

"Nothing fatal." I stroked a hand across Nugget's back. "How do you three feel about having a magic boost? We're in need of some serious crowd control."

"Point me in the right direction, and I'll make sure they don't get anywhere near you," Hilda said.

I lifted Russell from my jacket and placed him on my shoulder. "You good, Russell? Are you ready to be my flying gladiator?"

He flapped his wings and cawed.

I pressed my finger to their heads in turn.

They shuddered and bounced away from me as the magic covered them.

Nugget turned into a sleek, glossy giant cat with huge fangs. Russell exploded into an enormous silky crow with giant talons and a wicked sharp beak. Hilda, as usual, became a magnificently terrifying spider with giant fangs that rubbed together menacingly.

A wave of terror flooded across the crowd as they spotted my super enhanced familiars heading their way. Several groups broke away and fled into the gloom. Others stood there, shock on their faces as they took in my awesome giant familiars.

"Get to work, you three," I said.

They bounded away, chasing away the villagers and filling the air with growls, hisses, and roars.

I took a few seconds to admire my incredible familiars. I was so fortunate to have them.

Storm jumped off the witch pyre, and I grabbed Odessa's hand and helped her as we slid down the pile of smoldering wood.

I turned and looked back at it. "That was too close. If we hadn't—" I was slammed off my feet as something hot and spiky hit my back.

I landed on top of the pyre and lay there stunned for several seconds.

"I see him!" Odessa yelled.

I rolled over and discovered her firing magic at my attacker.

"We've got some heroes trying to make a name for themselves." Storm's hands were ablaze with sparks of lightning magic.

I jumped up and joined them. In front of us were two warlocks and four witches. They all looked young and angry as magic sparked on their fingers.

"I don't know any of them," I said. "What have they got against me?"

"I expect they've all heard the rumors about you," Odessa said. "That's all they need to fire them up. That and a little of the darkness that's troubling everyone."

"They're children," Storm said. "They're nothing to worry about. And they should respect their elders."

"You're saying we're old?" I said.

She shot out a spell, and it took one of the witch's off her feet. "I'm saying, we have experience."

"Go carefully with that experience," I said. "Remember, no fatalities in this fight."

There were several screams from the darkness. My familiars were doing their jobs well.

"We're not afraid of you," one of the warlocks said. He couldn't be more than twenty. "We know all about you, and you don't belong here."

"I do. Witch Haven is my home. You're not scaring me away." I raised my hands, sparking a spell on my fingers.

A witch threw out a spell which skimmed over my head and tickled my skin.

Odessa squeaked and dropped to the ground as a blast of magic slammed into her.

"Storm, cover me." I knelt over Odessa. She was clutching her arm as a line of blackness snaked along her veins.

"He got me with a curse! That little creep. That's Zyler Darkmore's son, Nash. I never liked him. He takes after his dad. Too smug for his own good."

I glowered at the boy who'd attacked Odessa. "He should know better than to use a curse he can't handle." I wrapped my hand around her arm, blocking the curse from moving any further, then channeled in healing magic. I imagined the curse being drawn out through her skin and disappearing into the breeze.

Storm grunted as she fired out more magic. "How long are you two going to be? This lot have youth on their side and are casting spells without breaking a sweat."

"I thought you said they were nothing to worry about," I said.

She grunted again. "I'm not worried. I just don't want a magic hangover tomorrow because I'm having to do all the heavy lifting."

"Hey! I'm cursed down here," Odessa said.

"You're not, anymore. It's gone. The magic was unstable and came away easily." I helped her up.

"I'm still giving Nash a stern talking to about the improper use of curses." Odessa brushed down her clothes. "And I've got something that'll make him think twice about messing with me again." She stuck her fingers in her mouth and whistled, then stood with her hands on her hips, seeming oblivious to the magic battle going on around her.

I blocked several spells that headed straight toward Odessa. "What are you hoping will happen?"

"Just you wait. My boys won't let me down," she said.

"Your boys had better hurry." Storm grimaced as she parried a spell that made her stagger back. "These kids are blasting with abandon, and one of their spells will get through, eventually."

The ground beneath my feet rumbled. Was this another spellcaster after us, or something new to worry about?

My eyes widened as I spotted six angry looking scarecrows racing out of the trees and heading straight toward the magic users who were attacking us.

Odessa clapped her hands together. "There they are. Go get them, boys."

The scarecrows growled as they launched themselves at the spellcasters. The battle was brief and messy, with straw and pumpkin splattered all over the place in a matter of seconds.

I raised a spell to offer my assistance, but Odessa restrained my arm.

"There's no need for that. My boys love a good fight. Let them deal with the children," she said.

In less than a minute, our attackers were face down on the ground, and the remaining scarecrows stood over them.

Odessa raced over to the downed scarecrows and inspected each of them. "Indigo, I could do with some help. I need to get these guys to my repair room." She heaved a huge scarecrow who was missing a head over one shoulder.

I knelt next to another deflated scarecrow. "This one is pretty messed up. Maybe it's best if you leave him behind."

"No! They saved our lives. I'm not giving up on my wounded soldiers. Grab Marmaduke and follow me."

I rolled him onto his back. Marmaduke was missing an arm, half the stuffing from his middle, and his head, but he was still twitching. Whatever magic was keeping him alive was intact.

I glanced up to see one of the scarecrows watching me with a creepy intensity. I raised a hand. "Hey. Thanks for the save."

He nodded and tipped his straw hat at me.

Storm strolled over and helped me to get Marmaduke balanced on my shoulders.

"That was too close for comfort," I said. "We were almost turned crispy and then bested by a bunch of teenagers with more attitude than sense."

"They didn't scare me," Storm said.

"And I know all their parents. If they'd gotten too feisty, I'd have dragged them home and made them explain themselves," Odessa said.

I nodded as I walked over to her. "We need to get out of here before more villagers arrive and pick up where their charming children left off."

"Let's go back to my place. I need to work on these scarecrows." Odessa looked at our six attackers who were still on the ground. "You know, I've often wondered what would happen if you combined a warlock and a scarecrow."

I snorted a laugh as fear darkened our assailants' eyes. "Sure. We could try that. This lot won't object to being willing subjects."

"Do you really think so?" Odessa grinned at me.

"Don't encourage her. She wasn't making a joke," Storm whispered in my ear. "Odessa really does want to try that out some day."

My laughter died. Odessa could be scary for someone so sweet and usually away with the pumpkin fairies.

"Um, we can't keep them," I said. "But we also can't let them go."

"Get these things away from us." Nash kicked out at one of the scarecrows. "I'll report you all for this."

"You can try, but your daddy won't help you now," Storm said.

"And you're in a world of trouble for blasting me with that curse," Odessa said. "My arm still stings. I should let my scarecrows eat you. A fat, tender morsel like you would be popular. They could share your limbs between them, and then—"

"No! We're not feeding them to the scarecrows," I said.

Nash scowled at Odessa. "My curse wouldn't have killed you. Although maybe it should have done, especially since you're hanging around with her." He glared up at me.

"You behave yourself, young man, or you'll be doing work experience with my scarecrows,"

Odessa said. "They like to knock sense into green beans like you."

"We could give them all a memory wipe so they don't remember the fight," I muttered. "And then your scarecrows can watch over them until we get out of here."

Odessa nodded. "That's a good idea. And my boys usually follow orders. I'm seventy percent sure they won't kill them."

The creepily intense scarecrow who'd been watching me, looked at me again and grinned. At least, it could have been a grin. Or maybe it was a snarl. There were a lot of sharp crooked teeth on display.

"What's with that one?" I said to Odessa.

"Oh, ignore Shamrock. He's lonely. And he's looking for love."

My eyebrows shot up. "With a witch?"

"Don't tell me you're biased about scarecrows?" Odessa said.

Storm chuckled. "Let's split. We need to lie low for a while until the dust settles."

"And figure out our next move," I said.

Odessa spent a minute giving her scarecrows instructions, so they'd guard the magic users until we were out of range of their spells.

The scarecrows all nodded along as she talked, although Shamrock kept glancing my way. I hoped he wasn't getting a crush, or he'd be disappointed. I wasn't into the country boy look, or straw, or pumpkin heads. Although I liked pumpkin pie. No! I wasn't going there.

"All set," Odessa said. "I'll cast the memory wipe spell, and these little darlings won't recall a thing about this evening."

"Great." I adjusted the scarecrow over my shoulders and turned to leave.

Three members of the Magic Council appeared out of the darkness. One stepped forward, his face partially concealed by the broad-brimmed hat he wore.

"Stop right there. None of you are going anywhere but jail."

Chapter 18

I glanced at Storm and Odessa, who stood either side of me. "Who are you? And why do you think we should go to jail?"

"Because you're criminals." The guy who'd spoken walked closer. "I'm Devlin Goody. And you're in breach of multiple Magic Council regulations."

Storm groaned and nudged me. "Devlin oversees magical compliance in this region. From what I hear, he's a stickler for the rules."

"Help us," Nash said, his voice an irritating whine. "They're trying to kill us with these insane scarecrows."

"Don't you go telling lies," Odessa said. "My scarecrows don't kill unless I tell them to. Usually. Well, almost never."

"Maybe you shouldn't go saying that out loud," I whispered.

Odessa lifted her chin and stared at Devlin. "We're the ones who've been wronged. We were drugged, put on top of a witch pyre, and almost killed. When we got away, this group came back and fired spells at us. We're the innocent parties."

"If you're friends with Indigo Ash, there's nothing innocent about you," Devlin said. "You'll all be arrested and questioned. And we already have enough on Indigo to detain her indefinitely."

"No way," Storm said. "You're not taking Indigo. She's served her time."

I caught hold of Storm's arm and gently tugged her back before she used her clenched fists on Devlin. "Storm and Odessa are innocent. They had nothing to do with any of this."

"I don't believe that," Devlin said. "You only have to look around to see how much magic has been used here. The place reeks of spells. And everyone knows these scarecrows come from Odessa's family farm. They wouldn't be here if she hadn't summoned them."

"You know about my work?"

Devlin nodded at Odessa.

"They're one-of-a-kind wonder scarecrows," she said sweetly. "I can fix you up with a real good deal on one if you need anything scaring away. I'll even throw in a batch of my special spiced pumpkin muffins since I'm in a good mood, being that I didn't get burned at the stake, and all."

Devlin glowered at her. "Bribes don't work on me. You're all coming with us."

I stepped forward. "Wait. They had nothing to do with this. It's all my fault."

Devlin tilted his head, a gleam in his eye as if he'd just spotted a toy he wanted to steal off someone. "I'm listening. What do you want to confess to?"

I set down the scarecrow I held. I looked at my friends and smiled. They weren't going down for this. "I used dark magic to compel Storm and Odessa to help me. They wouldn't have been here for any other reason."

"What are you saying?" Storm whispered.

"I'm saving you," I said.

"Don't be an idiot," Odessa said. "You know we'll always help you."

I turned to face them and kept my voice low. "The Magic Council doesn't have to know that. If you keep quiet, you'll be in the clear." I turned back to Devlin and saw him smirking. Maybe I should let Storm loose on him if he was going to get all smug about this capture.

"We always knew you'd slip up. Now you've just confessed in front of three members of the Magic Council about your use of illegal magic. Your time here is over, Indigo Ash. You're to come with us and be turned into a shadow," he said.

Odessa gasped. "You can't do that. Indigo is helping this village. You can't take her away and strip her of her powers. That's cruel."

"And we know our rights," Storm said. "There needs to be a trial and a judge to decide Indigo's fate. Not some jumped up little jerk in a too big suit who has an over-inflated opinion of himself."

Devlin waved a hand in the air. "That would be a waste of time. Indigo's actions have long been debated by the Magic Council, and we all know what needs to be done. Even if we went through the sham of a trial, the outcome would be the same. Her powers would be taken. It's the right thing to do."

I felt a slither of confidence grow as Odessa grasped my hand. Storm pressed against my right side, fury radiating off her. They were great friends, but I had to protect them. They'd stood by me even when I didn't deserve it, and then I'd gotten them shoved on a witch pyre.

If they kept helping me, they may lose their freedom. And there was no way they were sacrificing themselves for me.

"I could set my scarecrows on them," Odessa whispered.

"You could, but that would only buy us a little time. We need a more permanent solution," I said.

"It could be enough. We can get away and figure out how to make this right. Petition the Magic Council to ensure you get a fair hearing, and this idiot has nothing to do with it," Odessa said.

Something huge crashed through the trees toward us. Nugget leaped out, skidding to a halt beside the Magic Council members. He snarled at them, and they scattered in all directions.

Russell and Hilda were right behind him. Russell took to the air and dived after them, while Hilda growled and rubbed her fangs together.

Nugget's fur bristled as he stared at the pale faces of the Magic Council members. He turned to me. "What are they doing here?"

"They're here to arrest us," I said.

"Do these... these beasts belong to you?" Devlin swiped a hand down the front of his shirt and grabbed his hat, which had fallen off when he'd run away. "They're not natural. They must have been created by magic."

"Top marks for pointing out the obvious," I said. "They're my familiars, so they're full of magic."

"No witch should have familiars this large or this dangerous," he said. "It's yet more proof of your illegal use of magic."

Hilda advanced on Devlin.

He squeaked and backed away, magic sparking on his fingers. "Call it off, or I'll have no option but to destroy it."

"Don't touch a hair on my wonderful familiar's body," I said. "Hilda is a loyal and trustworthy familiar. And she's worth a thousand of you. You hurt her, and you really will see me use illegal magic. It'll be aimed right at your heart, and I won't stop using it until you're no longer moving."

"Did you hear that?" Devlin turned to his watching colleagues. "I just received a death threat from the Ash witch. She continues to condemn herself."

They both muttered their agreement, although neither looked comfortable about being here.

I resisted the urge to roll my eyes. "What did you expect me to say? You threatened my familiar. Hurt her, and you hurt me. And Hilda's done nothing wrong to you. She was protecting me from an attack by the villagers."

Russell swooped over Devlin's head several times, making him duck.

"Call them all off, immediately." Devlin backed away until he was standing by his colleagues.

It was so tempting to let my familiars loose on the Magic Council employees. They wouldn't stand a chance, and it would give us an opportunity to escape. But what then? I'd be in even more trouble for using my familiars to attack people. And that may lead to them being taken away, too. I couldn't let that happen. Not when they'd been so loyal to me.

"Get over here, you three," I said. "They're not worth it."

Nugget stalked around the group several times before returning to my side.

"How did you get on with chasing away the villagers?" I stroked a hand through his thick fur.

"No one died, but everyone was terrified. They'll think twice before shoving us onto a witch pyre again any time soon."

I gave his side a pet, before stroking Russell, and then giving Hilda a quick tickle under her enormous belly.

"It's time we destroyed the source of all our troubles," Devlin said. "Everyone is convinced you're the reason this village has become unstable. We get rid of you, and life can return to normal."

"I used to think that could be true, but it's not so simple," I said. "If I come with you, will you listen to my side of the story?"

"I've no doubt your side of the story is full of lies and deceit," Devlin said. "And we have enough evidence to charge you with several magical infractions. And you've broken the rules of your probation. There's nothing you can say that'll make any difference."

"Don't be so quick to make assumptions, Devlin." Olympus stepped out from behind a tree.

Devlin's mouth opened and closed several times before he snapped to attention. "I didn't know you were still in the area. I thought you'd gone back to the headquarters."

"Then you thought wrong. I've been monitoring the situation in Witch Haven ever since Indigo's return." Olympus strode over.

I tried to get a read on his expression, but his face was blank. He excelled in hiding his emotions.

"We were alerted to a disturbance," Devlin said. "We arrived to find Indigo and her associates attacking some villagers. We were just about to arrest them."

"You need to check your facts," Storm said. "We were defending ourselves."

"You were being influenced by a powerful force. A force I intend to have destroyed," Devlin said.

Olympus raised his hand, a flash of annoyance crossing his face. "I'll make sure a suitable punishment is administered for the crimes committed here."

"But... I found her," Devlin stammered. "I mean, we arrived in time to see the crimes happening."

"You big fibber!" Odessa said. "Unless you were hiding, you were nowhere near the witch pyre."

Devlin glanced at his colleagues, his cheeks flushing pink. "We observed from a safe distance. But that's not the point. The evil Ash witch also admitted she wanted to harm me with dark magic."

"The evil Ash witch is called Indigo," Olympus said.

"Of course." Devlin nodded at me, hatred burning in his eyes. "Indigo."

I raised my eyebrows. Why did Olympus care how I was spoken about? I'd been called a lot worse than evil.

"Your involvement in the arrest will be noted in my report," Olympus said. "But these matters need to be handled discreetly. And if you were paying attention to your surroundings, you'd have seen we have an audience."

I looked around, and sure enough, a few villagers had returned and were watching the action from the trees.

Devlin scowled for a second, then nodded. "Of course. As you wish. You're in charge."

"It's important that things are done correctly. If anything goes wrong, I'd hate for it to be a bad mark on your service record," Olympus said. "I believe you're up for a promotion. Assistant director of magical compliance? You wouldn't want anything to tarnish your chances, would you?"

Devlin blinked rapidly. "I didn't know you were aware of my application. This arrest would help me secure the position."

"I'm aware of everything that goes on in my area of the Magic Council." Olympus nodded at him. "This won't be forgotten, but I'll take over from here."

"Is Limpy going to let us go?" Odessa whispered. "You're buddies now, aren't you?"

"I really have no idea when it comes to Olympus," I said.

He looked over at me. "You're to come with me. The others can go free."

Devlin looked like he wanted to protest, but clamped his lips together and decided to give me his best scowl instead.

"You're still arresting Indigo?" Odessa said. "Why?"

Olympus ignored the question and gestured at me. "We can do this the easy way, or the hard way, but it's happening. You need to explain what happened here."

"We can help with that," Odessa said. "Take us, too."

"Keep quiet," I muttered. "This is your chance to get away. We still have to find Luna, and we can't do that if we're all locked up."

"But... what about you? We don't want you locked up either," Odessa said.

"It won't be the first time, and I can handle it." I glanced at Olympus. At least I hoped I could. I had no way of knowing which direction this would go. I sort of trusted Olympus, but the last time we'd spoken, we'd parted on bad terms. Would he hold that against me?

"We'll take her," Devlin said. He nodded at his companions. "She won't cause us any trouble."

"No. I'll deal with Indigo's transportation. This has been my case from the start, and I intend to finish it," Olympus said.

Devlin glowered at him. "As you wish."

"Make a record of events here and send me your report," he said.

"What about the other witches, and those... things?" Devlin gestured at my familiars.

"Odessa, Storm, and the familiars are to go free. Take their statements, but that's all. Let's move," Olympus said to me.

Odessa wrapped me in a huge hug. "I don't like this. I wish you'd let us help."

"You can help by staying free and working on finding Luna."

Storm leaned over and gave me a fist bump.

I looked at the chaos I was leaving behind. Anyone who stumbled on this scene would see some big magical business had gone down, and I was smack bang in the middle of it. There was no getting away with this.

Nugget growled and head-butted me with his huge, sleek furry head. "I could always bite Olympus' head off for you. That would stop him."

Hilda wrapped a heavy, hairy leg around my shoulders. "Don't do that. I have a good feeling about him. And he won't be so handsome if he's missing his head."

"Take care, you three," I said. "Hopefully, I'll be out as soon as possible and we can continue looking for Luna."

Nugget head-butted me again so hard that I almost fell over. Russell tapped the top of my head and cawed, while Hilda tightened her hold on me.

"I'll be fine. Don't worry. Just hang out at the house until I get back. And no heroic moves like last time."

"You just say the word, and we'll come for you," Hilda said. "Nothing will stop us from getting you out."

Olympus loudly cleared his throat.

I patted Hilda before heading over to Olympus.

"I'm glad you've seen sense," he said. "Let's get this over with."

"I'll come with you, but I'm not going down quietly. We were attacked. Albert Black drugged us, and the villagers—"

"Just keep quiet. It doesn't matter what you say to me now. Your fate is sealed."

I glowered at the smug Devlin as I walked past him. It really seemed like my freedom was gone for good.

Chapter 19

"Since you want this done quickly, and for me to be a quiet, well-behaved witch, why not simply transport us back to the Magic Council?" I trudged alongside Olympus as we headed away from my friends and familiars.

"Why would I waste my magic doing that?" he said. "Dematerializing two people isn't done with a simple click of the fingers."

"So you can get that gold star and pat on the head you've been wanting so badly for finally putting me back behind bars. Surely, that's worth one little transportation spell. I'm not walking all the way."

"You're right, you're not." Olympus didn't speak again until we were well away from the trees and anyone who might try to listen in. "I'm taking you back to my office, not a Magic Council meeting."

I shrugged. "I guess you have a lot of paperwork to process after arresting a dark witch."

"I usually do. Keep walking and hurry. The slower you go, the longer this will take, and the Magic Council hate it when I bill them for too much overtime."

"I'm messing up your budgets," I said. "My heart bleeds for you."

He slid me a glare and picked up the pace.

Unless I wanted to blast my way out of this with more magic, I had no choice but to follow him. And I'd accepted I had to take this punishment, so long as Odessa and Storm went free and my familiars were unharmed. And I knew they'd make sure Luna got home safely. Everyone would be okay. Well, everyone except me.

We reached Olympus' office fifteen minutes later. He unlocked the door and ushered me in ahead of him.

It was the same blank, soulless little place I'd seen a few days ago. There wasn't even a pot plant to brighten it up. There was just a desk, a couple of chairs, and a pile of files, no doubt holding the latest information about the criminals he wanted to track down.

I turned to him. "So, what now?"

Olympus paced in front of the large window in the office. "I've been investigating."

"Isn't that your job?"

He raked a hand through his hair. "I've been looking at the journal you gave me. I read Magda's entry. And I read other information in there. She was troubled before she was arrested."

"That's news to no one. What's your point?"

He stopped abruptly and turned toward me. "My point is, you could be right. Witch Haven is in trouble."

I narrowed my eyes. "Do you think it's a trouble of my making?"

"At first, I thought it had to be you. It made sense."

"It never made sense to me. And I had no idea about the problems Witch Haven faced until I came back. I'm not the witch in control of this darkness. Although..."

"Although what?"

"I wondered if turning up in the village made things worse. Or it accelerated the problems people are dealing with."

"Perhaps you stirred a few things up," he said, "but what if this is bigger than you?"

I nodded, hope blooming in my chest. "It is! That's what I've been telling you. The evil hauntings, Luna being taken, the villagers misbehaving and trying to burn me and the others. Witches don't burn other witches."

He shook his head. "Things should never have gone that far. Who led on the attack?"

I shook my head. "It doesn't matter who was the ringleader. What matters is the villagers aren't acting in their right minds. If they keep on like this, there will be more deaths."

Olympus narrowed his eyes. "Storm said you were drugged. Who did that to you?"

I let out a sigh. "Albert Black, but he was acting so strangely, I should have known something was wrong with him."

"What was he doing that was so strange?"

"He was happy to discover Luna is dead. And he doesn't care how it happened."

"Wait! I've not heard about this. How do you know that?"

"There's a lot you missed out on after you stormed out of Ursa's house."

He grumbled under his breath. "So tell me. I'm listening."

"I tried to summon a ghost with Storm and Odessa, but we got Luna through instead. Or at least it looked like Luna. I'm not convinced anymore that it was her, since she was also acting strangely."

Olympus held up a hand. "One startling new revelation at a time. Is Luna alive or not?"

"I'm going for alive."

"Even though you saw her spirit?"

"We saw a spirit that looked like her, but it didn't act like her. Not entirely. Something is playing with us."

He nodded slowly. "And the ghost summoning? What was that all about?"

"I was attempting to prove Ursa stole a ghost jar from my house. It contained one of the ghosts that had been haunting Luna."

"Ursa stole from you?"

"Possibly. Again, I'm not so sure anymore." I wasn't sure about a lot of things, including what Olympus had planned for me. "All I can say with some certainty is that Witch Haven has gotten weird. And that weirdness isn't of my making."

He turned and looked out the window. "I agree. The number of strange hauntings have grown, and residents have been acting oddly for some time. And not just in their usual quirky ways. There have been some nasty cases come across my desk in the last few months. People attacking each other with magic, damage done to properties, and then there are all the fires. It's as if they're trying to destroy this place. Or ensure that—"

"Or ensure someone destroys it for them," I said. "That's the direction the Magic Council is heading. You said they were taking a vote on whether to raze the village to the ground and relocate everyone. The darkness manipulating this place wants everything out of control. When it's all messed up, it'll be easy to sneak in and launch a coup."

"You think it's the dark witch coven?"

"What else can it be? It's not me. It's not anyone else I can think of. We need to find out who is in this coven and stop them before it's too late to save Witch Haven."

"It may already be too late to save the village." Olympus continued his pacing.

I watched him, my initial hope wavering. Could I ever trust him? Most of his life, he'd been involved with the Magic Council, and it must tear him apart that he was having doubts about how effective they were. They'd missed a takeover bid happening under their noses. But were those doubts enough to get him on my side? Did I even want Olympus Duke on my side?

He turned back to me. "The last time we met, I reacted badly."

"That's an understatement. You strangled me because I stopped you stealing Mary-Sue."

His forehead wrinkled. "Yes, and I didn't mean to do that. I lost control. It won't happen again."

I needed to cut him some slack. He'd lost a child. I had no clue how that felt, but it must be horrendous.

"And I didn't mean to be unsympathetic about what happened to your daughter. Honestly, I was shocked when I found out about Bloom. Odessa told me what happened. I wish I could have been around to help."

Olympus slumped against the wall, suddenly looking ten years older. "Her disappearance always felt off to me. And she would never have gone off with a stranger. She was a smart child and knew better than that. And even though things weren't great between me and her mother, we always taught her the right values to live by."

"It wasn't your fault," I said. "You thought she'd be safe. After all, she was surrounded by law enforcement."

"It is my fault. Bloom was my responsibility. She still is. I still believe she's alive and out there somewhere. I should never have left her, but I was so caught up in that case, trying to prove myself. It seemed like the most important thing." He shook his head. "It shows what I know. It also shows that I should listen to other people more. I'm not... I'm not always right about things."

"What it shows is that you're the same as all of us. We make mistakes and don't always get things right. I know that first-hand."

His expression was troubled when he looked at me. "If what you're telling me about Magda is true, and there is a dark witch coven out there, you're also not to blame for what happened all those years ago. You were a teenager when Magda got herself in trouble. You didn't even have your full powers. There was nothing you could have done to stop the dark magic from infecting you. Magda should have known better."

"Magda was protecting me. She'd have done anything to keep me safe. She was trying to do the right thing. And she trusted this coven. Maybe that makes her naïve, but it doesn't make her a bad witch. Just like you leaving Bloom outside while you looked at a crime scene doesn't make you a bad parent, or responsible for her vanishing."

The pain in his eyes cut straight through me. "I don't know. Perhaps you're right. And perhaps I need to be more open-minded about what happened in your past. You did your best, but you couldn't control the magic, so bad things happened. You didn't wilfully attack the villagers."

I glanced at the floor. "At the time, it felt like I was doing it willingly. It wasn't until I learned about the possibility of dark magic being involved, that I doubted I was all bad, and that maybe I could be a better witch. I really didn't see a future for myself until I came back to Witch Haven. Actually, I didn't want a future. I didn't think I deserved one."

He let out a soft sigh. "Indigo, never give up on yourself."

"Really? I sometimes think I should. You've read the file on me, so you know what I did. And I believed it all for such a long time. It wasn't until I returned here and saw my old home again, my friends, and realized I could be useful, that something clicked into place. I wanted to try again. I wanted to right the wrongs I'd inflicted on Witch Haven."

Olympus' expression was hard to read, but it looked like he might believe me. "And I think that's what you're doing, in your own law breaking fashion."

"I'm trying to, but it's difficult. I've spent a long time not trusting anyone and thinking I could do things alone."

"And how's that been working out for you?"

Since we were having a share your feelings moment, I laid all the ugliness on the table. "It made me lonely, jaded with the world, and wanting to give up."

"You're too young to be jaded," he said.

I grinned at him. "I'm not that young. I'm old enough to know better. I'm also old enough to admit when I'm struggling. It's not always easy to get things right, but I've found that having my familiars and my friends beside me has literally saved my life more than once since I've returned. I don't want that to change. And I really don't want to lose my powers just as I'm finding my feet again."

Olympus went quiet once more. "You should be punished for breaking the rules."

"I only bent them a tiny amount. You'd have to really pay attention to notice what I did wrong."

"You snapped the rules in half."

"I was doing good. Doesn't that give me leeway?"

He gave me a half smile. "I always find it better if you don't do things on your own, especially not when it comes to complicated magic. And I definitely never want to hear you've been tackling this dark witch coven alone. They seem immensely powerful with no scruples, and they wouldn't think twice about destroying you."

"I've got no plans to do that. I'll need all the help I can get to take them down." I sucked in a breath and took a risk. "If you let me keep my powers, maybe we can work on this together."

Olympus narrowed his eyes. "You trust me enough to work with me?"

"I'm... I'm learning to. You've stood up for me twice now. And you could have let Devlin and his goons take me away. Instead, you put your neck on the line."

He pursed his lips, and so many emotions flashed across his face that I couldn't read them all, but I thought I spotted hope in his eyes.

"My motives for considering working with you aren't entirely selfless," he said.

"I don't care what your motives are, so long as you're not sending me back to prison." My magic pulsed inside me, eager to break free now it was on the brink of no longer being restrained and under scrutiny.

"I need power on my side. You're a powerful witch, and I can sense the magic vibrating off that necklace you're wearing. Was that one of Magda's creations?"

I touched the necklace and nodded. "My magic has been evolving ever since I got back. I think it's got something to do with this. My spells are still on the rusty side, but they're improving every day. And now I'm trusting myself more, it doesn't feel like a struggle to use my powers."

"Good. Because I need those powers." Olympus walked over to the desk, lifted a piece of paper, and handed it to me. "I got this yesterday."

I took the piece of paper and read the words on it. *We have Bloom. If you want to see her alive, you'll do what we tell you.*

My mouth opened, and I stared at him. "Is this for real?"

Olympus shook his head. "It can't be. It's some sicko who heard about Bloom going missing and wants to play a joke on me. It isn't the first time I've gotten a messed up message like that."

"You can't ignore it. What if it's legit?" I turned the paper over. "Have you got any idea who sent it?"

"No. It was pushed under the door when I arrived this afternoon. I ran a tracing spell on it, but whoever left that message knows what they're doing. There's nothing there to tell me who wrote the note and who left it for me to find."

"Olympus, this is incredible. Aren't you excited? Bloom's alive. This is proof."

"It's proof of nothing, other than that people have twisted minds."

"If you're not going to investigate this, then I will. What if this message is genuine? Someone could be holding Bloom, and you could get her back."

"So long as I do what they tell me," he said. "Doesn't that remind you of something?"

"Magda's journal entry! The coven insisted she help them or I died. You don't think they have Bloom? The witches are looking for a new puppet to play with?"

"It crossed my mind. And this would be a strong way for the coven to infiltrate the village."

Coldness flooded through me. "If they got a powerful member of the Magic Council on their side, they'd be unstoppable. You know all the secrets of Witch Haven. You could let them in, and no one would be able to stop you."

"I could definitely do that."

My heart skipped a beat. And not in a good way. "Would you do it, if it meant you got Bloom back?" This was a horrible dilemma for Olympus to face. If my child went missing, I'd do anything to get her back, maybe even do the bidding of this coven.

"I wish I could tell you with any certainty that I'd have nothing to do with their devious plans, but I'd be lying." He walked over and caught hold of my arm. "Which is why I can't investigate this on my own. And I can't rely on the Magic Council. If they hear I'm receiving messages like this, they'll take me off the case. They won't trust me."

"Does that mean you want us to work together? I can help you find Bloom."

"I need a magic user who doesn't mind bending the rules. It's not so easy for me to do, given my position."

"I'll do it! I'll snap those rules so hard they won't be able to remake them."

A smile lifted one corner of his mouth. "Hopefully, it won't go that far. But if Bloom is out there..."

"We'll find Bloom and Luna. And we'll bring down this coven." My magic sparked heat in my chest. "I've already tried locator spells to find Luna. They didn't work, but we could try the same thing for Bloom. Or we could—"

"No! I've tried every magic spell I can think of to locate Bloom. Whoever has her, if they do even have her, they're too smart to be tricked by a spell."

"So... what do you want to do?"

He faced away from me and then turned back sharply, his expression dark. "The right thing. I'm a key part of the Magic Council. I can't be seen to let them down, even if Bloom has become entangled in the darkness damaging this place."

I stared at the magic sparking on his fingers and took a step back. "What does that mean for me?"

"It means you need to close your eyes, Indigo."

I blinked at Olympus. Had I failed to convince him? Didn't he love his daughter enough to keep searching for her? Was he going to strip me of my powers right here and now?

I held up my hands. "Wait! Let's at least talk about this. I can still be useful to you."

He shook his head. "Do you trust me?"

"I... I kind of." This trusting people business was so new to me that it was scarier than one of Odessa's scarecrows on a mission to slay.

"Then close your eyes, and let's see how far I can stretch that trust," he said.

"If you kill me, I'm coming back from the dead and haunting you for the rest of your life. And I won't be a friendly ghost. I'll be a slime slinging, banshee howling, icicle forming nightmare of a spook."

"I'm not going to kill you. But shut your eyes so you don't get dazzled. And this magic is complex, so don't fight it."

I took a huge breath, closed my eyes, and hoped that whatever he was about to do would be over fast.

Chapter 20

"You look the part, but I can't get the voice spell right. Why do you still sound like you?" Olympus stood in front of me, a frown on his face.

"It's not my fault your magic keeps going wrong. And I'm still not sure about this." I turned and looked in the full-length mirror in the back room of Olympus' office. A different person stared back at me. Gone was the purple hair, my familiar face, and my casual clothing. I'd been replaced by someone who wore lots of dark leather, had inky black hair, and wore way too much eyeliner for my liking.

"It's been three days. You must be used to your new look by now. I need to figure out why the voice spell won't take, though. You must be fighting my magic," Olympus said.

"I'm not fighting you!"

"I suppose there's a first time for everything."

I pursed my lips. "I can't get comfortable looking like someone else. Let's try something else. How about you purge my record so I can wander around Witch Haven a free person? Then there'll be no need for this disguise."

"Not a chance. Even I don't have that much clout in the Magic Council," he said. "This disguise has to work, especially now most of the villagers are on the hunt for you, plus my colleagues in the Magic Council, and this mysterious dark witch coven. You have to keep a low profile. Your life depends on it."

"And what's more low profile than being a completely different person." I shook my head at the stranger in the mirror.

Olympus' transformation magic still made my skin tingle and itch. It was a combination of strong, intoxicating spells. I should be grateful for what he'd done. Instead of turning me into a shadow and taking my powers, he'd transformed me into every warlock's naughty dream. I was now masquerading as a leather-clad ghost hunter with a pout and too tight pants. It was taking some getting used to.

"This is perfect. I've been discussing with the Council about getting a new ghost hunter in post," he said. "And you fit the bill. Plus, you know your way around the spirits. I've already filed the appropriate paperwork, so your details are with the Magic Council, and—"

"I'm getting a real job at the Magic Council?" I grinned at him. "Does that mean I get a pay check, too?"

"Do you need one?"

"Desperately. A witch cannot live on air and handouts from her friends forever." I smoothed my hands over the leather. It did have a pleasing stretch to it. "Talking of payments, I have a confession to make."

"What's that?"

"After I spectacularly failed to deal with Ursa's hexed house problem, she still paid me, minus a damage fee. Did you come to some private arrangement with her? I didn't think the Magic Council took on private jobs."

He groaned and shook his head. "She's always doing that. And it's not a payment, Ursa's basically attempting to bribe me. She gives out what she calls little bonuses to keep us on side. I know of several employees at the Magic Council who take that money. I hope you didn't accept it on my behalf."

"Um, maybe I did. If you have a problem with keeping the money, you can donate it to me. Call it a sign-on bonus for my new job. And I'm a very good cause. Plus, if you expect me to strut around in all this leather gear, I need a decent incentive to show my face to the world."

"You don't like the leather? It's durable, and it's breathable. It's regulation issue for all our hunters."

"It makes me look like the Wiccan version of Catwoman. All I need is the pointy ears and a tail."

He chuckled. "That can be arranged. You'd look cute with a tail."

"Don't you dare." I ran my hand over my newly colored hair. Although it was a shock to discover what Olympus had done to me, it had a logic to it. He could introduce me around the village as his new pet ghost hunter, and I'd be free to investigate Luna's disappearance, what happened to Bloom, and figure out if the note he received was connected to the dark witch coven.

"Let me try that voice changing spell on you again," Olympus said. "We don't want your voice giving you away."

"You shouldn't bother. I've been away for such a long time, not many people know what I sound like," I said. "And I've avoided most of the villagers since coming back. Although I'll need to be careful around my familiars, Storm, and Odessa. They'll know me."

"You need to stay clear of all of them," he said. "This is our secret."

"I should keep them involved. They could be useful."

"Don't worry about that. They're keeping themselves involved, despite me telling them to stay away."

I chuckled. My friends and familiars had been pounding on the door on a daily basis, demanding to know what had happened to me. So far, Olympus had fobbed them off, but he'd have to give them a straight story soon.

It made my heart ache to leave them out of this, but maybe it was for the best. I'd gotten them in heaps of trouble since I'd returned. If I wasn't around, I couldn't get them hurt anymore.

Olympus placed his hand over my throat and spoke the words to evoke the voice change spell.

He stepped back and his gaze ran over me. "Say something."

"You're a jerk for making me keep this a secret from my best friends."

"That's better. You'll need to practice. And walk around a bit. You've got a distinctive strut, and I don't want that to give you away."

"I don't strut. I walk like a normal person."

He arched an eyebrow. "You definitely strut. Go on. Do a circuit of the office so I can watch you."

"You sound like a dirty old man."

"I'm not old."

I snort laughed as I did a turn around the office, making sure not to strut.

I'd been staying in Olympus' back room ever since he'd come up with this plan. There was no funny business going on, it wasn't that kind of arrangement. He'd moved into a short-term rental nearby. We were keeping this strictly professional.

It was weird spending so much time with someone I'd considered my enemy until a few days ago. But then, that was my life. One big ball of messy, magical weirdness.

I missed my old home and wanted to get back there, but I had to stay away until this mystery was solved. Well, mysteries. Every time I felt like I was making progress with Luna's disappearance, another layer of complication was added. Hexes, hauntings, disappearances, evil-eyed villagers. What next, the dead rising and chasing me out of here?

Maybe I'd be forever struggling through these puzzles and having to stay in disguise as... I turned to Olympus.

"What's wrong?" he said.

"I need a new name to go along with my new look."

"I've been thinking about that. How about Sally Snow?"

I wrinkled my nose. "It doesn't fit the image. All this leather and the crazy amount of eyeliner calls for a kick butt kind of name. How about Neon Daggerthrust?"

"Never in a million years. You could be Daffodil Meadow."

"That's ridiculous. It's even worse than Sally Snow."

"I'm coming up with names that are the opposite of Indigo Ash."

"We should stick to something that sounds the same but different."

"If you make it too similar, people could see through the illusion."

"How about Indy Archer?" I said. "That way, I won't ignore someone when they call my name and I'm not in character. Sometimes, I was called Indy when I was a kid."

"You don't think that's too similar?"

I shook my head. "I doubt people will put two and two together."

"It could work. But keep out of the way of Storm, Odessa, and your familiars. They might recognize the name Indy and start poking around and asking you awkward questions."

"I have to at least check in on them. They could be making progress with Luna's disappearance and have useful information I've missed."

He crossed his arms over his chest. "If I tell you no, you'll only do it, anyway."

I grinned at him. "You know me so well."

"If you keep tabs on them, do it from a distance. No making contact. And I'll be sure to check in on them, too, to get any updates."

I chuckled. "They'll love that."

"They won't have a choice but to accept it. I can claim I'm making inquiries to discover your whereabouts. Now, strut over to the table and take a seat. The pancakes should be ready."

I tossed my head back and deliberately stomped to the table.

I didn't like to admit this, but it was weirdly nice to be in Olympus' company. The more time I spent with him, the more I liked him, which was as scary as a haunted house on the stroke of midnight on the winter solstice.

I had to get a grip on this liking Olympus business. I wasn't in Witch Haven to find a guy who would sweep me off my feet, I was here to right wrongs, help lost loved ones, and restore order to my home and family name.

I settled in my seat as Olympus tossed pancakes and placed them on pre-warmed plates.

I may not be looking for love, but I was still a hot-blooded single woman, and Olympus was a decent looking guy. If I did nothing else, I could enjoy the view of a guy making me pancakes for breakfast.

He walked over with a stack of pancakes for us both. He placed them down, then grabbed the coffeepot and some maple syrup, before settling in his own seat.

"I had no idea you were so domesticated," I said.

"You get used to doing things like this when you live on your own," he said.

"I was more of an order in kind of girl when I lived alone."

"You never found a decent, non-magical user to spend your time with?" He drizzled maple syrup all over his pancakes.

"I wasn't interested in finding anyone to flip my pancakes. I just wanted to keep my head down and watch the time pass by. If I hadn't come back here..." My words trailed off. I'd been in such a dark place, so full of self-regret and loathing that I'd lost sight of everything I'd had in my life.

Olympus reached over and touched the back of my hand. "I get it. We've had different experiences, but I do understand your loss. You were close to Magda, and when everything went wrong, it must have been a terrible wrench to lose her. And to have dark magic infect you and not understand what was going on must have been confusing."

I nodded, almost too caught up in my own head to notice he was still holding my hand, but not quite. It felt good. It had been a long time since a guy had held my hand. I could get used to it.

"I guess we have that in common," I said.

"Maybe we have more things in common than you realize." He grinned, withdrew his hand, and attacked his pancakes.

"Olympus, I want to thank you."

"For the pancakes? No worries."

"No, not for these, although I expect they'll taste great." I set down my knife and fork. "You're risking everything by doing this. If the Magic Council find out you're helping a witch on their most wanted list, you'll be history. Everything you've worked so hard for will be taken away from you."

He lifted one shoulder. "It's taken me a while to figure this out, but my career isn't my life."

"It sort of is, though," I said. "When we met, I could see how driven you were. You only cared about catching me and sending me back to jail. Nothing else mattered."

"That was my only focus. But that was before I got to know you. You're different to how I expected. And everything I thought I knew about Witch Haven is different, too."

"I won't let you down. You've got a lot riding on this, just like me. And we will find out what happened to Bloom."

Olympus went to reach for my hand again, when a loud knock on the office door made him jerk back.

"You need to hide," he said. "We haven't figured out your full back story, and I don't want anyone to find us before we're ready to release you on the world."

I grabbed my pancakes and coffee and raced into the back room.

Olympus nodded at me, then headed to the door and opened it.

I peered through the crack in the door and stifled a groan. It was Ursa.

"Good morning, Ursa." Olympus' tone highlighted how displeased he was to see her.

"I've had another sleepless night," Ursa said.

"Did you have a hot date?"

"Hot... how dare you!"

I pressed my mug against my mouth to stop from laughing. Who knew Olympus had a sense of humor?

"My apologies. Have your gnomes been misbehaving again?" he asked.

Ursa cupped her hands under her bosom. "No, it's not the gnomes, they've been less troublesome. They seem preoccupied by something. And they keep laughing for no reason. Something's going on with them."

I grinned as I ate a pancake. They should be laughing. I'd snuck out last night and delivered them their first batch of honey mead. No doubt, most of them were nursing sore heads after a raucous night of celebrating with such a potent alcoholic drink. I'd gotten tipsy on just the fumes.

"So what's the problem? I'm assuming you're here because you're unhappy about something," Olympus said.

"Too right, I'm unhappy. The hex hasn't gone away."

I wrinkled my brow. Those hexed dolls were still playing up? I figured Storm had smashed most of the troublemakers to pieces. Whatever hex was in Ursa's house was more potent than I'd realized.

"I'm not sure how I can help. The assistance the Magic Council has already provided hasn't worked," Olympus said. "Perhaps you should hire a private contractor."

"It only failed because you used a corrupt witch to deal with my issues," Ursa said. "Indigo was useless. And I'm so glad to hear she's gone. I've been speaking to some of the other residents, and it sounds like they ran her out of the village after scaring her with that witch pyre. It's an excellent outcome. We don't need bad sorts like that ruining things."

"You agree with burning witches?" Olympus almost growled out the words. "Don't you know that's illegal?"

"Oh! Well, of course I do. And they'd have never gone through with it. But it made Indigo see she's not welcome here." Ursa's cheeks flushed.

They had meant to burn me. My feet had been toasty warm as the flames licked toward me. I'd be nothing but a charred witch if I hadn't escaped with the others.

"If Indigo caused the problems in the village, why is your house still hexed?" Olympus said.

Ursa pressed her lips together. "It must be the dark residual energy she left behind. After all, she slept in my home. I've arranged to have it cleansed. In the meantime, I insist you make my hex a priority to investigate. I need my rest."

"I'll put it on my list, but there are more pressing matters in the village I need to deal with."

"That's not acceptable. I demand you make me a priority, or I'll lodge a complaint with my uncle. I'll tell him how unhelpful you've been. Aren't the elections coming up soon? You don't want to lose your position."

I finished my pancakes, licked my fingers clean, and did a final check of my new appearance in the mirror. Yep, I still looked like a scary-eyed ghost hunter in a too tight leather outfit. I may as well try out my new disguise.

I stepped into the office and strode over. Maybe I strutted a little for Olympus' benefit. "Hi, there. I hear you have a problem with a hex."

Ursa blinked at me several times. "And who are you?"

I stuck out my hand. "I'm Indy Archer. The Magic Council's new ghost hunter."

She reached over and gave my hand a limp shake. "This is the first I've heard about your employment."

"I literally arrived five minutes ago. Olympus wants to make sure you receive the best experience from the Magic Council, so he only employs the most qualified magic users. How may I help you?"

I didn't miss the way Olympus glared at me, but I was done hiding. I had my disguise in place and I had to get to work.

"I hope you're suitably experienced," Ursa said. "I've had enough broken promises from the Magic Council."

"I've had more experience with hexes, spooks, and hauntings than you've had hot dinners," I said. "I'm sure I can deal with your problem. Did you mention a hexed house?"

Ursa gave a nod, before launching into a long-winded explanation of her hex and how badly her nerves were affected.

I nodded along with her, making noises in the right places. There were so many problems in Witch Haven, so I may as well start with this one.

I'd miss having Storm and Odessa around to help, and hated that I couldn't see my familiars, but once

I solved the mystery of what was troubling Witch Haven, I'd get them back, and that included Luna.

And while I was tackling those issues, I'd also work on restoring my reputation and making sure Magda's name was cleared.

This mission wouldn't be easy, but I was determined to make things right.

Ursa drew in a breath.

I grabbed her arm and hustled her out of the office. "This sounds like a delicate matter. Let's go see about your hexing problem, shall we?" I winked at Olympus, before leading Ursa away.

He opened his mouth as if he was about to protest, then sighed and nodded.

I turned as I reached the end of the street. He was still watching me. I raised a hand to him.

What we were attempting was a crazy long shot, like trying to perform a transformation spell when you only had half the ingredients and were missing your spell book. There was a high chance we'd lose it all. But I was willing to give this everything I had to make sure Witch Haven remained safe, and my friends were back by my side, where they needed to be, and where I needed them.

I wasn't giving up on my home, no matter the sacrifice I needed to make.

About Author

K.E. O'Connor (Karen) is a mystery author living in the beautiful British countryside. She loves all things mystery, animals, and cake.

If you want to be part of the Witch Haven crew, practice spells, solve a few murders, spend time with amazing witches and their talking familiars, and get a **free** book, join her weekly newsletter.

Every Thursday you'll get news on the mysterious happenings in K.E. O'Connor's world.

Sign up today.

Newsletter:
https://BookHip.com/QKGDWJW
Website:
www.keoconnor.com/writing
Facebook:
www.facebook.com/keoconnorauthor

Also By

Spells and Spooks
Hexes and Haunts
Curses and Corpses
Muffins and Moonlight
Cupcakes and Cauldrons
Pancakes and Potions
Hauntings and High Jinx
Hauntings and Havoc
Hauntings and Hoaxes
The Case of the Screaming Skull
The Case of the Poisoned Pumpkin
The Case of the Cursed Candy
Fire Fang
Silvaria

If you enjoyed

Hexes and Haunts

turn the page to read an extract from the next Witch Haven mystery

CURSES AND CORPSES

ISBN: 978-1-915378-30-9

Chapter 1

I paced the wood paneled corridor in the Magic Council office for what felt like the hundredth time. Whenever an employee walked past, I tensed, worried they'd see through my magic disguise and have me arrested.

"Will you stop that?" Olympus Duke muttered. He was lounging in a chair by a set of large sturdy double doors, his eyes half-closed.

I frowned at him. He looked like he didn't have a care in the world and wasn't about to go in front of high up Magic Council employees with me by his side.

Olympus pointed to the chair next to him. I shook my head. He may be able to play it cool, but I was a wanted witch, wearing a complicated magic disguise. And if that disguise broke, I'd be in a whole heap of trouble.

"Indigo, come sit next to me," Olympus snapped. "You're only drawing attention to yourself."

I wiped my sweating palms on the back of my leather pants and perched on the seat next to him.

I jumped up a second later. "There's serious power behind those doors. What if someone sees through this magic? They could see who I really am."

"Then we'll both be in trouble if that happens. But it won't. You talk as if you doubt my ability to hold your disguise in place."

I glanced at Olympus. He was tall, dark, and handsome in an uptight way. He was also the Head of the Magic Council, and until recently, had been gunning for me. Now, we were on the same side, but I had no clue how long that would last.

He arched an eyebrow as he caught me studying him. "You doubt me?"

"I doubt everyone, myself most of all." I stared down at my clothing, still not comfortable in my disguise. But this was the only way I could freely move around Witch Haven, without the villagers or the Magic Council pointing the finger and hunting me down.

"We won't be in there for long. They have a fifty point agenda to get through today, so won't have much time to spend on you."

How anyone would willingly work for the Magic Council was beyond me. All those meetings and official rules they needed to abide by would drive me crazy.

"I'll do the talking," Olympus said. "You simply nod and say yes or no at the appropriate time. This is a rubberstamp exercise. They just need to make sure you're fit for duty."

I nodded as I chewed on my bottom lip. I'd give a heck of a lot to have my familiars with me. Nugget would be hanging around my neck and smart talking Olympus, Hilda would be reassuring me as she tap danced on my shoulder with her spidery legs, and Russell would be flying around and making people duck as he dive bombed them.

But I was on my own. In this disguise, no one would figure out I was really Indigo Ash, a failed witch with a murky past. I needed to remain in this disguise until I figured out a way to get my best friend, Luna Brimstone back, then clean up my dubious reputation and that of my stepmom, Magda.

I turned on my heel and almost walked straight into Olympus.

He caught hold of my shoulders. "Take a deep breath and relax. A sweating top lip is attractive on no one, not even you."

I scowled at him and dabbed my top lip. My fingers came away damp. "You'd be anxious too if you were in my position."

He pointed at my mouth. "Keep that shut, nod and smile, and we'll be out of here in no time. Then we can get back to focusing on what's important."

Olympus was right. There were a ton of important things to get done. I had to find Luna, but there was also the not insignificant issue of a dark witch coven infiltrating my wonderful home of Witch Haven. That was also on my list of problems to sort out.

I took in a deep breath and let it out slowly, hoping it would send me to a calmer place.

"That's it. You're doing great."

I nodded and stepped back from Olympus. My opinion of him had changed dramatically over the last week. Initially, I'd hated him. He represented everything I despised. But there was more to him than being an uptight employee of the Magic Council. He had depth, and a tragic past that haunted him. He was also an amazing pancake maker and had a sense of humor, which I was only just discovering.

The more I learned about him, the more I liked. And that was also something to worry about. With so many complicated things to tackle, a tricky romance with the enemy didn't need to go on my list.

The double doors we waited beside were pushed open. "Olympus Duke and Indy Archer." A small, stout elf wearing a stiff collared shirt and green pants looked at us.

"That's us," Olympus said.

"Please, follow me."

"Just remember, play it cool," Olympus muttered as he followed the elf into the chamber.

I cleared my throat and shook out my arms. I could do this. So long as I didn't make any smart comments, we'd be fine. This was going to be a challenge.

I'd been in front of the Magic Council recently, but for a different reason. They'd planned to try me for magic crimes and strip me of my power. But it would be different this time, I hoped. I really hoped it would. I couldn't afford to mess up anymore.

The chamber was full of various members of the Magic Council. They all looked thoroughly bored, and several were asleep.

Presiding over the meeting was a judge I'd met before. Judge Zimmerman was an elderly warlock who radiated power.

He gestured us to a table in the center of the chamber. "Olympus, it's good to see you again. I hear you've been successful in your recruitment of our new ghost hunter."

Olympus inclined his head at me when I lagged behind, so I sped up and plastered a smile on my face.

"That's right. Let me introduce Indy Archer. She came highly recommended and has a knack for communicating with the dead. Given the situation in Witch Haven, she's well-placed to make inroads into the troubles in the village."

Judge Zimmerman peered at me for several long, uncomfortable seconds. "That sounds excellent. And I hear you've already been dealing with a perplexing matter already."

I glanced at Olympus, and he gave me a nod. "You mean Ursa Wyrm?"

"I do. I was speaking to her uncle yesterday. Apparently, Ursa hasn't made a complaint to him in two days. You've done the impossible. You've made her happy."

There were several chuckles from around the chamber.

"I'm glad she was satisfied with my work," I said.

"We are all very satisfied. We're happy to have you join us. May I ask how you dealt with the problems Ursa was having?" Judge Zimmerman said.

I hesitated. Ursa's creepy manor house was far from cleansed of the dark energies and misbehaving spirits that swirled around it. It was hardly a surprise that Gravesend Manor was so troubled, given the place was built on an old graveyard. But I'd found a compromise. A way to keep the troubles and spirits occupied. And that compromise involved the gnomes who lived in Ursa's yard.

Olympus nudged me.

"I communicated with the appropriate energies, and learned of their concerns," I said swiftly. "We came to an arrangement. There may be one or two bumps in the road to iron out, but Ursa shouldn't have any new complaints to bring your way."

"I wish I could believe that. But for now, we're all grateful she's no longer a problem. Long may it last."

There were several muted cheers from around the chamber.

"Indy's work with Ursa was a test of her abilities," Olympus said. "And with your permission, I'd like to make her trial with us permanent."

"I should think so too," Judge Zimmerman said. "With everything that's been going on in Witch Haven, we need all hands on deck. Get right to work, Miss Archer. Welcome to the Magic Council. Olympus will deal with the required paperwork and your salary."

I grinned at him. "Thanks. I look forward to getting my next assignment."

"Very good. You may both leave. Now, let's see what's next on the agenda." Judge Zimmerman leaned over his paperwork.

Olympus gestured me away from the table, and I was happy to hurry out and have the doors shut behind me. It felt like I'd escaped something dangerous.

I breathed out a sigh as we dashed down the stairs and smiled at Olympus. "We did it. We deceived the entire chamber. All those magic users and none of them saw through the disguise."

"You're a genius." He arched an eyebrow. "Anyone would think you have a powerful magic user on your side who created that disguise you wear so well."

I laughed, partly in relief, as we walked along the corridor. I was no longer tense now I'd survived trial by a bunch of bored magic users. "It makes me think the Magic Council isn't that powerful."

"Meaning?"

"Meaning, no one saw through your magic. None of them are that strong. It's all a front to keep other magic users from misbehaving."

Olympus glanced around and then leaned closer. "Don't get too cocky. My magic transformed you, that's why no one saw through the disguise." He wriggled his fingers and magic sparkled in the air. "They wouldn't have just anyone heading up this place. I have serious skills."

"You're very sure of yourself," I said. "No one makes perfect magic."

"I've always been sure of my magic. If you doubt your ability, it'll go wrong." Olympus gave me a meaningful look.

I glanced away. I knew what he was getting at. When I'd arrived back in Witch Haven, I'd had zero belief in myself or my ability to use magic safely. Therefore, what I believed in came true, and every spell I cast had malfunctioned.

I brushed my fingers over the powerful amethyst necklace I wore. Things were changing. And my magic was changing too. So was my belief in myself.

"I have to ask, how did you deal with Ursa's problem?" Olympus said.

We reached the main doors of the building, and a security guard let us out.

"It was easy. I used honey mead."

"You got Ursa drunk?"

I chuckled. "No, but I did a deal with those gnomes who wanted you as their sacrifice. In exchange for a regular supply of honey mead, they're happy to go dark energy hunting. And they love chasing down those evil dolls Ursa insists on keeping. So I arranged for a bunch of merry gnomes to maraud through the place every night and take out the worst of the energies. And it's working. I dropped by to see Ursa just this morning, and she was almost nice to me."

"Wonders will never cease. Ursa Wyrm being a decent witch." Olympus smiled and shook his head. "I'm glad you figured something out."

I stopped walking and turned to face him. "So, now my disguise and my employment as a ghost hunter is official, how about we focus on finding Luna?"

"I have no problem with you doing that. But you also have to look like you're working for the Magic Council."

"And I agreed to do that. I have my disguise on and my magic is primed. I'm just waiting for my next assignment. What will we be doing?"

Olympus worked his jaw from side to side. "We're not doing anything. You'll be working solo."

"Oh, okay. What will you be doing?" It wasn't like I cared. I was used to working alone.

He narrowed his eyes a fraction. "I have business to attend to outside of Witch Haven."

I looked away and frowned. I shouldn't mind that Olympus wouldn't be around. We were still working out what kind of friendship we had. Or even if it was a friendship. Maybe it should be described as more of a twisted business arrangement with a high likelihood of failure and death.

"I won't be gone long," he said. "And as you've pointed out, your magic is firing on all cylinders, so you'll have no concerns about handling a case on your own."

I shook away any thoughts that I'd miss him while he was gone. "You can count on me, boss. But I need to make time to find Luna. It's one of the reasons I agreed to keep this disguise, so I can move around freely and figure out who took her."

"I haven't forgotten. You can work on locating Luna in your free time. But I've already got a new assignment for you, and that needs to be your priority until I get back."

I clasped my hands together. "Please let it be a cute missing magical creature, something fluffy that likes snuggles and doesn't put up a fight when I hunt it. Something that won't blast me to pieces and then eat my bones."

He snorted a laugh. "I doubt these particular creatures will want to eat your bones, but there are no guarantees. I haven't seen them in action."

This didn't sound promising. "What evil critter have you got for me to deal with?"

"I've had a complaint from our Cemetery Guardian, Silvaria Digby. Apparently, the dead are rising."

"Rising as in coming back as ghosts?"

"No, it's more basic than that. Corpses are rising from their coffins and wandering around the cemetery."

"That's... disturbing."

"It is. So far, Silvaria has kept them contained in the cemetery, but the numbers are literally rising. She's unhappy and needs a solution. Your job is to investigate what's making them reanimate and then get them safely back in the ground."

"They're not angry, zombielike corpses, intent on eating my brain, are they?"

"Silvaria made no mention of any attempts at eating brains." Olympus checked his watch. "Go up to the third floor to get the details. There's a file waiting for you."

I glanced back at the building we'd just come out of. "You want me to go back in there alone?"

His smile was sly. "You're a bad, bold witch. I thought you could handle anything."

I grumbled under my breath. "Of course I can."

"Then what are you waiting for?" Olympus said.

"Nothing. I'm just..." secretly afraid of the Magic Council? Wanting to go anywhere but back inside that creepy building on my own? Nervous Olympus will drop my disguise when I'm in a room full of Magic Council employees and leave me to fend for myself because I've annoyed him too many times?

He gave my arm a brief squeeze. "Off you go. I'll be back soon. You can tell me all about the fun you had with the corpses. And keep an eye on Silvaria. She's been working as a cemetery guardian for a long time."

"That's a bad thing?" I'd never met Silvaria Digby.

"Being around dead bodies all the time changes a person."

"Is she dangerous?"

"Anyone with power over the dead is dangerous. Don't expect her to be friendly. She prefers the company of the dead to the living."

"Duly noted. Don't annoy the Cemetery Guardian or she'll set an undead horde on me."

"That's about the size of it. I'll see you soon." He stared at me for a second, then turned and walked away.

I watched Olympus go. He was a strange one, and I had yet to figure him out. He had a foot in two camps. Olympus was committed to the Magic Council, but I sensed an unhappiness in him when it came to his work. He'd also suffered loss and blamed himself for that. There was more to him than just a stuffed shirt Magic Council official. But I needed to make sure I didn't get distracted by poking about in his complex life. I had to focus on finding Luna and clearing my family name. And neither of those things would be easy.

I turned back to the building and reluctantly went inside. I slowed at the end of the corridor by the main staircase as two familiar voices drifted toward me. My eyes widened as Storm Winter and Odessa Grimsbane march past and up the stairs.

I looked around to see if anyone was paying me attention and then followed them. From the angry looks on their faces, they weren't here to make friends.

This day had just gotten a lot more interesting.

Curses and Corpses is available in e-book and paperback

ISBN: 978-1-915378-30-9